ROBERT THE BRUCE

BY

ERIC LINKLATER

WITH A FRONTISPIECE AND TWO MAPS

PETER DAVIES LIMITED

1934

First published in May 1934

Printed in Great Britain for PETER DAVIES LTD. by T. and A. CONSTABLE LTD.
at the University Press, Edinburgh

TO

DOUGLAS WALKER

TO RECALL SOME HIGHLAND FORAYS AND TO
CELEBRATE A LONG TREATY OF FRIENDSHIP

The Frontispiece is a photograph of the cast of the skull, generally supposed to be the Bruce's, discovered and re-interred at Dunfermline in 1819. The cast is in the Scottish National Portrait Gallery.

NOTE

THE principal sources of information upon the life and wars of Robert the Bruce are the Documents relating to Scotland edited by Joseph Bain ; Barbour's poem, *The Brus* ; the contemporary Lanercost Chronicle ; and *Scalacronica* (1355-57), by Sir Thomas Gray of Heton.

In addition to these there are two modern historical studies of such importance as to require special mention : *The Battle of Bannockburn*, by W. Mackay Mackenzie, and *The Scottish War of Independence*, by Evan Macleod Barron. Dr. Mackay Mackenzie discovered the true site and elucidated the true manner of the battle of Bannockburn : Mr. Barron, in addition to clarifying the sequence of events in the War of Independence, established the importance, previously neglected, of the part played by the Highlands of Scotland in that war.

To both these gentlemen I wish to express my indebtedness and my gratitude.

MAP OF SCOTLAND

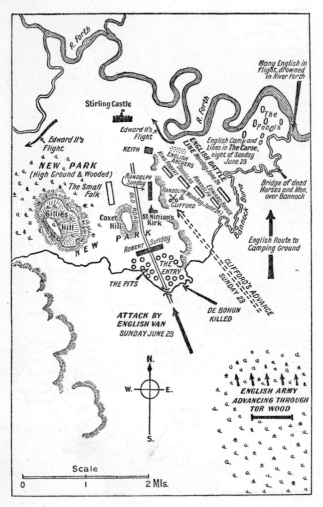

MAP OF BANNOCKBURN

I

*For as much as it is delectable to all human nature
to read and to hear these ancient noble histories of
the chivalrous feats and martial prowess of the
victorious knights of time past* . . . So Lord
Berners begins the prologue to his translation
of *Petit Artus de Bretaigne*; and so, with some
blotting of the adjectives, might one begin
to write of the adventures of Robert the
Bruce were there not, in this year of doubt,
some disinclination to regard the life of action
—and especially military action—as a life of
unequivocal merit, and a certain tendency to
look sideways on tales of the shedding of blood
and the dealing of hard blows unless some
excuse more valid than the *brio* of chivalry
can be adduced for their companion pictures,
insistent though unrecorded, of the pains of
death and defeat.

To a simple vision, to a schoolboy or
romantic vision, the story of Bruce, from the
day he murdered Comyn to that Spanish
morning when the Good Sir James, impatient
of Alphonso's tardiness, rode headlong into

the Moorish host of Granada, bearing with him the Bruce's heart, his own still faithful, has on the surface of its brave events glamour enough to make any protestation of its significance, or explication of its value, seem unnecessary as the botanist's name for a rose. Simply as a tale of adventure it is more worth the telling—to those who find pleasure in tales of adventure, that is—than all your histories of Huon of Bordeaux, Palmerin of England, and the knights-errant, mythical or real, whose valour produced the renaissance of heroism that preceded (and quickened perhaps) the renaissance of learning. It is a tale of steadfast endeavour, a tale of perilous feats and brilliant escapes, of littleness growing to greatness, of the magnanimity of friends, of high purpose and of lasting courage, of success in the end and the sweet recognition of success by an exhausted enemy. Its pattern might have been designed for an epic poem : for it begins with a desperate foolhardy blow, it crowns a king who has no kingdom to match his crown, it puts him to flight and makes him a homeless wanderer, it tries his spirit with hardship and defeat, it gives him a dozen exploits of the kind that legends are made of, and slowly it gives him a little success against his foes ; he takes a castle or two, he gathers friends, he adds another hillside to his kingdom, and Scotland comes to life again ; then Edward his brother, that reckless man, throws down the gage to Edward of England, Bannockburn is won, and the *de jure* King of Scots is King *de facto* after eight years of fighting ; but the tale is not ended : the independence of his country is not yet acknowledged, the fact of his kingship is scarcely admitted, his right to the throne is still suspect abroad ; so the war goes on ; Randolph and Douglas, the twin paladins of Scotland, hammer the northern counties of England as England once hammered Scotland, and Scotland is filled with a new pride and the certainty of victory ; the nobles and the people of Scotland publish, in rude and magnificent words, their declaration of independence ; the Bruce is their sovereign lord, generous, honoured, and beloved. Then at last England admits, the Pope acknowledges, his title and Scotland's ; and now the King bids Douglas prepare to carry his heart against God's enemies, since all Scotland's are beaten, and, as if waiting only for that latter consummation, though piously remembering the former claim, in peace gives up the ghost.

So much for high adventure. John Barbour, Archdeacon of Aberdeen and the Bruce's first biographer, wrote his history in burly octo-

13

syllabics that sometimes build their roughness into poetry ; and a better poet might have made of the same matter a better poem : for the Bruce's story is the very stuff of heroic poetry.

But poetic celebration of soldierly achievement, even with all the trappings of romance, is not so sweet on the world's palate to-day as once it was. We desire, at the least, the visible ordering of a dramatic situation ; we like to mix a little psychology, a few problems of character and ambiguities of conduct, with our vicarious adventure ; behind the exploits of an individual we look for political or economic significance ; we are often dubious about the validity of national sentiment, and so we prefer a patriot to be—as well as a romantic warrior—a kind of footnote upon patriotism ; and we read our history with a new and vivid sense that time is a factor at least as important as any Stuart, Plantagenet, or Bourbon who ever lived.

Now the story of Robert the Bruce fulfils all these requirements. In his adventurous uphill path to Bannockburn, in the following period of consolidation and ceaseless warlike importunity of acknowledgment, and in his death so closely following acknowledgment, there is a simple dramatic shape ; in the emergence of national sentiment, released by his endeavour,

there is the mainspring of drama ; and the
time factor, that decreed the death of
Edward I and the succession of a very different
king, introduces a third dramatic element.
The nature of the action, the sentimental im-
pulse behind a great part of the action, and
the accidents of time are congruent, and
bestow on the drama a clearly discernible
pattern.

There is also, in the story of Bruce himself,
an apparent mystery, and in the history of his
opponents there is a psychological curiosity.
After the murder of Comyn in the church at
Dumfries, Bruce is the very exemplar of a
patriot : before the murder he was alter-
nately friend and false friend to King Edward,
false to Scotland when Scotland's cause was
Balliol's cause, and true to no one but himself.
Why, then, should this notable example of tergiversation suddenly become a model of steadfast idealism ? The answer, the only answer,
is that he became true-bound to Scotland when
he could identify Scotland's good with his own.
When Balliol's cause was lost and when the
Comyns were discredited, when the murder
of the Red Comyn compelled him to win
Scotland or die as Wallace had died, then
Bruce turned to Scotland and declared himself a Scot for the last time. He had chosen
his nationality deliberately, years before the

death of Comyn, but he declared it in desperation, and with a compulsory gesture of defiance he became a patriotic king. As soon as he could hope to say—this year, next year, some time, ever—*l'état c'est moi*, he became loving and leal to Scotland, and as a consequence of this noble enlargement of selfishness he rescued Scotland from a servile estate, he re-created its spirit and established its freedom, its independence, on a foundation that endured four hundred years. In a national estimate he is the greatest of the few great Scots, and the fundamental selfishness of his patriotism does not belittle him : for though the poor man, the little man, the common man may sometimes be moved to fight and die for his country without hope of reward, the great man is never passionately a patriot until he can say, in some degree, as Bruce could say in the highest degree, *l'état c'est moi*.

Now consider the psychological curiosity, common but still entertaining, on the English side : Edward I, that stern and soldierly man, died and was succeeded by Edward II, that post-war young man. How time brings in its revenges, and how revolutionary are the hereditary fruits of blood ! The Bruce was a great man, being great in himself ; he is great in history because of that intrinsic greatness and also because the tide of the years was with him and he rowed to fortune on its flood. Had Edward I been a milder man, Scotland would not have been driven to heroic desperation, Edward II might not have been driven to seek amusement in the whimsical company of Piers Gaveston, and, with peace at home, the military virtues of the Bruce might have sent him to seek glory in a crusade. But the weakness of Edward II, that was the heritage of Edward I's oppressive strength, was the Bruce's opportunity, and being great he used it.

There remains, in this examination of the Bruce's eligibility for modern attention, the effect of his career upon his own country and his own people. And here one is tempted to be extravagant, and may indeed yield to extravagance without offending the truth. For under his leadership Scotland displayed a national sentiment whose lofty passion is for evermore the honour of Scotland, and whose assertion of a nation's right to freedom is a notable clause in human nature's claim to nobility. Not seldom has a country cried for freedom ; less often its people have achieved it ; but never has a country, never have people more passionately insisted on freedom, as it were a cardinal thing in life, as it were bread or water, than did the Scots in the first quarter of the fourteenth century. They had the will for it before Bruce joined them, but it was he who gave them the voice to demand and the strength to exalt it. ' It is not Glory, it is not Riches, neither is it Honour, but it is Liberty alone that we fight and contend for, which no Honest man will lose but with his life.'—So spoke the nobility and people of Scotland, in the year 1320, in their remonstrance to the Pope.

From his uncle, who was a priest, Sir William Wallace had in his boyhood learnt the tag, *Dico tibi verum, libertas optima rerum,* and under Bruce's leadership the creed became a battle-cry and a triumphant cry.

Forty years after his death—forty years more or less—Barbour wrote :

> ' A ! fredome is a noble thing !
> Fredome mayss man to haiff liking ;
> Fredome all solace to man giffis :
> He levys at ess that frely levys !
> A noble hart may haiff nane ess,
> Na ellys nocht that may him pless,
> Gyff fredome failythe : for fre liking
> Is yharnyt our all othir thing.'

That belief was the Bruce's legacy, as freedom itself had been his gift to Scotland.

II

In the year 1290 the Maid of Norway died in Orkney. She was about eight years old. She had been Queen of Scots since the death of her grandfather, Alexander III, in 1286, and she was on her way home to a kingdom already divided by faction when she fell ill and died. Had she lived she would have been married to the Prince of Wales, for Edward I had secured a papal dispensation for this union, so agreeable to his imperialistic ambitions, and the Guardians of Scotland had consented to it.

But she died, and the union of England and Scotland was indefinitely postponed. Her death caused great confusion, for Alexander's line came to an end in her, and in many households there was an eager rustling of pedigrees, an earnest computation of whatever royal blood had come in, whether below the blanket or above it, and a dozen claims to the throne were prepared and supported by tales of dubious descent from improbable monarchs. But the more sagacious claimants

19

made friendly overtures to the English king, whose influence was greater than any family tree, though its roots had gone down to Gaidel himself and Scota, the Pharaoh's eponymous daughter.

Edward was invited to arbitrate. He accepted the invitation and exploited it. He came in as arbitrator and went out the accepted Overlord of Scotland. The regents acknowledged him, the nobility acknowledged him—there is a rumour that the *communitas* protested—and the Competitors swore fealty to him as Lord Paramount. The competition for Scotland's diminished throne was a wordy scramble, void of dignity. Only two of the Competitors had claims that seriously demanded consideration, and these were John de Balliol and Robert de Bruce, Lord of Annandale and grandfather of the Bruce who became king. Both showed descent in the female line from David, younger brother of William the Lion : the former was David's great-grandson through his eldest daughter ; the latter, a grandson through his second daughter, pleaded his claim by virtue of the Scottish custom—that possibly did not exist—to prefer the senior generation. Edward decided in favour of Balliol, who was crowned at Scone in November, 1292.

Now the Bruces had entertained a royal ambition before they submitted their claims to open competition, and this ambition was fairly well grounded, for in 1238 Alexander II, an old man who had prematurely abandoned hope of fathering a son, had with the consent of the *probi homines* declared the Lord of Annandale to be his heir. This decision, however, he subsequently invalidated by begetting a child of his own. But the Bruces did not forget it, and shortly after the death of Alexander III they attempted, without much success and without any regard for the Maid of Norway, to seize the kingdom for themselves. Their attempt found little support apparently, for they did not persist in it, and their infant war soon died. But their ambition lived on. At the first rumour of the Maid's death the Bruces armed and came in arms to a Council sitting in Perth. Frightened by this spectre of war, Bishop Fraser of St. Andrews wrote to Edward and prayed him to come northwards, as far as the Border, ' for the consolation of the Scottish people, and the saving of the shedding of blood.' He included a delicate warning against the machinations of Sir John de Balliol—' we advise you to take care so to treat with him that in any event your honour and advantage be preserved '—and concluded with the courteous prayer that Edward might enjoy ' long life, health and prosperity, and happiness.' Edward, indeed, was already in

21

a very happy position. All the Scottish fortune-hunters, privily and discreetly, were seeking his aid and warning him against their rivals. Already his cupboards were lined with pledges, like a pawnbroker's in the first week of a coal-strike. And his own ambition was greedier than that of any Bruce or Balliol, and more adroitly planned.

Having chosen Balliol as Scotland's king, Edward immediately began to make life—a kingly life—impossible for him. Balliol was summoned to London in respect of appeals taken to Westminster from the Scottish courts; he was summoned to London to answer for a wine-bill left unpaid by the late king, Alexander; he was ordered to serve on the justice eyre of Yorkshire, as though he were one of Edward's minor barons; he was commanded to attend the English king on the latter's campaign in Gascony, though Balliol's absence from Scotland, at that time, would beyond question have seriously endangered his already precarious tenure of the throne. And, of course, his refusal to accompany Edward was fatal to him. Balliol, with good sense but ill luck, had concluded a private treaty with the French king : but that was small protection against Edward.

Alternative inferences may be drawn from Edward's treatment of his Scottish nominee :

either he was endeavouring, without loss of time, to reduce Scotland to the status of an English barony, or he was deliberately driving Balliol to rebellion. If the latter inference is correct, Edward succeeded. Balliol rebelled and banished all Englishmen from his court, and seized their property. The Bruce was numbered among these ' Englishmen,' and his estates were given to John Comyn, Earl of Buchan. Edward mustered a great army and marched to Scotland. He besieged Berwick. His fleet suffered a serious repulse, and his army was infuriated by the barbed invective of the garrison. The walls of Berwick, however, were hardly so robust as Scottish wit, and the English army soon entered the town. By Edward's orders no quarter was given to the townspeople, and eight thousand were massacred in three days of busy discipline.

A month later Balliol was crushingly defeated at Dunbar, and Edward began a triumphal progress through Scotland, receiving everywhere pledges of allegiance and being assured by the nobles that they now repudiated both Balliol and the French alliance. Edward no longer dissimulated : he came openly as Scotland's master, as he had always meant to come. He seized the Stone of Destiny, relics such as St. Margaret's fragment of the True Cross, and as many national documents as

23

he could find. In 1296 he held a parliament at Berwick and nearly two thousand Scottish landowners and churchmen signed the Ragman's Roll and made submission to Edward as King of Scotland. Robert de Bruce, son of the Competitor, and Robert Earl of Carrick, the Competitor's grandson, were among the signatories. Scotland was on its knees, and to this undignified position it had been brought partly by Edward, partly by its own nobility.

Bruce the Competitor, an old man, had died in 1295. He had refused to do homage to Balliol and had surrendered his land in Scotland to his son, the second Robert. The second Robert, being also unwilling to admit Balliol's sovereignty, had transferred it to his son, the third Robert, who, since he took possession of it, had apparently fewer scruples and swore a timely allegiance. It was this third Robert, now Earl of Carrick and a bachelor of King Edward's chamber, who later became the Scottish patriot and king. In 1296, being then twenty-two years old, he was much favoured by the English king, and Edward went to some slight trouble to minimise for him the inconvenience of certain debts he had found time to contract : this was not an idle favour, but the reward of good service, for earlier in the year the Bruces, father and son, had been sent to their lands of

Carrick and Annandale—the lands which Balliol had recently confiscated—to receive their tenants and other men of those parts into King Edward's peace.

Edward left Scotland a sullen defeated land, with English garrisons in the castles, English sheriffs, English priests in many of the churches, and Surrey, his proconsul, in supreme command —to whom he made the pretty jest, '*Bon bosoigne fait qy de merde se deliver*.' That may be so, but he flattered himself in thinking he had got rid, so easily, of the filth he had been so eager to acquire. No matter what facile promises the *probi homines* had given, there were plenty of *improbi* Scots not yet resigned to English domination, and scarcely had Edward turned his back on the north to embark on another imperialist venture—Philip of France, as crafty as Edward himself, had recently cheated him out of half a dozen castles in Guienne—when rebellion flared and Wallace gathered the broken men of Scotland to fight for the liberty their betters had renounced.

Of William Wallace comparatively little is known, but his patriotism was a kind of genius. The English called him a brigand and described his adherents as felons. Nor is there any reason to suppose that his first exploits were on a larger scale than brigandage. But it was brigandage with a principle, and because the English oppressors were well hated the principle was a popular one, and Wallace's guerilla force grew in numbers 'as there flocked to him,' says Fordun, ' all those who were in bitterness of spirit, and weighed down beneath the burden of bondage under the unbearable domination of English despotism.'

Now Robert Wishart, the Bishop of Glasgow, was a fervent patriot and a sagacious man. He had, moreover, special cause for resentment against Edward in the latter's attempt to anglicise his Church by the presentation of English priests to Scottish benefices. He knew how superficial was Edward's conquest, and it seems probable that he kept in touch with the more sturdily resentful elements that existed in various parts of the country, and co-ordinated them for the widespread rebellion that broke out in the spring of 1297. He encouraged Wallace and made use, for the common good, of his growing influence. Before the end of May there was a large and successful rising in Moray, under Andrew de Moray, an able and energetic young soldier ; there was a rising in the neighbourhood of Aberdeen ; Macduff and his sons were out in Fife ; there was trouble in Galloway ; Wallace had killed the Sheriff of Lanark, and he and his ragged army, joined by Sir William Douglas, had marched to Scone and attacked the English justiciar ; and in the West the Bishop of Glasgow, the Steward of Scotland, and the young Earl of Carrick were in the field.

At this time the elder Bruce was Edward's governor of Carlisle, and the younger Robert —the Earl of Carrick—had recently been summoned there to reaffirm his allegiance to Edward before undertaking a small punitive expedition against the lands of Sir William Douglas. Having taken the oath and raided the Douglas acres, he promptly turned his coat and joined the rebels.

He excused his recusancy by declaring that his renewed fealty had been sworn under compulsion. That was probably true. Oaths of allegiance were the current coin of Edwardian politics, and they were generally extorted, by the force of circumstance or the cogent voice of opportunism if not by some sterner argument, and most of them were broken. They were merely a token coinage. Attempts were often made to strengthen the holding power of an oath by multiplying the sacred objects on which it was taken. For one whose word was suspect a few relics might be added to the Gospels : in 1300, for instance, the Bishop of Glasgow, an heroic perjurer for Scotland's sake, was persuaded to swear fealty to Edward on the Consecrated Host, the Gospels, the Cross of St. Neot, and the fragment of the

27

True Cross in the Black Rood of St. Margaret. Edward put a lot of trust in the authority of this remarkable relic, but Wishart was too accomplished a churchman to be trapped by inviolability, and he evaded the grip even of St. Margaret's Vera Crux. Bruce's evasion of the oath taken at Carlisle was much easier: he had been required to swear on nothing more serious than the Host and the sword of Becket.

Bruce's reason for joining the insurgents was in all likelihood a compound one: the excitement of rebellion, a patriotic infection, and the hope of setting himself or his father on the throne if the rising were successful. All these motives may have influenced him, the first two encouraging the last, and the last supplying material fuel for the others. But the venture had no success, and the army of the West capitulated without fighting to an English force, slightly superior in strength, at Irvine on July 9. The Scots were not yet in arms for Scotland—save those who followed Wallace—but for Bruce or Balliol, and Bruce and Balliol were irreconcilable. Wallace himself was then and always a Balliol man; Andrew de Moray, still in the North, was for Balliol, and so was Sir William Douglas; the Steward and the Bishop were of Bruce's party. And so, failing to decide for whom to fight, the army of the West did not fight at all, but surrendered. Wallace and his men retired and maintained their principles, though somewhat quietly, in Selkirk Forest. Douglas yielded with an ill grace : three weeks later, in prison at Berwick, he was still ' very savage and very abusive ' ; and after two years' imprisonment, recalcitrant to the last, he died in the Tower. But he left a son who lived to be known on the one side as the Good Sir James, and on the other as the Black Douglas, whose reputation is revealed, by a negative, in the English lullaby :

> ' Hush ye, hush ye, little pet ye,
> The Black Douglas shall not get thee.'

The sequel to his capitulation at Irvine was that the Bruce was ordered to surrender his infant daughter Marjorie as a hostage for his good behaviour, and the Bishop, James the Steward, and Alexander de Lindsay—another partisan—were in the meantime made guarantors of his loyalty. But Bruce did not surrender his daughter, nor did he re-enter the English fold for some considerable time. On October 13, 1297, the elder Bruce was dismissed from the governorship of Carlisle ; a month later a document issued from Westminster authorised the Bishop of Carlisle and Sir Robert Clifford to receive at their discretion the younger Bruce and his friends into the King's peace—but Bruce did not take advantage of this offer ; later in the year, and again in February, 1298, Clifford, the English Warden of the Western Marches, raided and burnt in Bruce's lands of Annandale ; and on June 4 the Bruce's property in Essex was seized to pay the debts of whose burden Edward had relieved him in October, 1296.

In the meantime Wallace and de Moray had gained their decisive victory at Stirling Bridge. De Moray unfortunately died of his wounds, but Wallace was hailed as the saviour and nominated the Guardian of Scotland, to hold and rule it for Balliol. His army received large reinforcements, Surrey retired to York, and Wallace, on his heels, invaded England and laid waste the northern counties.

Edward was forced to abandon his French campaign in order to deal with this nearer menace. He mustered a great army and in June, 1298, again invaded Scotland. Wallace offered battle at Falkirk, but his strategy was at fault and his simple defensive tactics included no guard against the English archers, who won a decisive and bloody victory. Having taken Stirling, Edward marched against the Bruce, who held Ayr and the West. Bruce burnt the castle of Ayr and retired into Carrick, whither Edward was unable to follow him, either because the English army was short of victuals or because the English nobles were unwilling to remain in the field for longer than the statutory forty days of feudal service. On his way back to England Edward captured the Bruce's castle of Lochmaben : so Hemingburgh declares, from whose narrative are taken the other particulars of Bruce's movements about this time.

In the summer of 1299, his influence at home diminished by his defeat at Falkirk, Wallace went abroad to enlist for Scotland the friendship of the King of France and the influence of the Pope. He had been superseded, as Guardian, by the Bruce and Sir John Comyn of Badenoch—the Red Comyn, that is, whom Bruce later killed in Dumfries— who maintained the pretence that Balliol was still the King of Scotland. They had already been in diplomatic communication with the King of France, and Philip had returned a sympathetic answer by the hand of Bishop Lamberton of St. Andrews. In August, 1299, at a conference held in Selkirk Forest, the Bishop was also made a Guardian of the realm, and to him was given custody of the Scottish castles ; the dynastic rivalry between Bruce and Comyn was clearly making their twin Guardianship a somewhat unstable combination ; the Comyns themselves had a claim

31

to the throne, but they were staunch supporters of Balliol, whose kinsmen they were.

The conference at which the new Guardian was chosen was an unruly affair. Among those present were John Comyn, Earl of Buchan ; the Steward of Scotland ; Sir Malcolm Wallace, William Wallace's brother ; the Earl of Menteith ; Sir David de Graham, one of Balliol's faction ; and the three Guardians. Graham took the opportunity of Wallace's absence abroad to demand his goods and lands, on the plea that he had left Scotland without permission. Sir Malcolm said this could not be done till it was decided whether he had gone abroad for the good of the country or against it. Then these two knights gave the lie to each other and drew their daggers. Now Graham had come to the conference with the Red Comyn, and Malcolm Wallace with the Bruce, so immediately a suspicion rose that the quarrel was premeditated : the Red Comyn ' leaped ' on his fellow Guardian, the Bruce, and took him by the throat ; and Buchan ' leaped ' on the Bishop, thinking treachery was planned. Fortunately the Steward and others stopped the scuffle before any serious damage was done.

In spite of this unfortunate beginning the new Guardianship endured, without further reported discord, till the early months of 1302, though there is reason to suppose that the Bruce's enthusiasm for the cause they espoused—the cause of Balliol—was dwindling towards the end of their association.

In the early days of their rule, however, the triumvirate was very active. Bruce carried war into the enemies' lines in Galloway, and, in November, Stirling Castle was besieged and presently captured. The Scots appeared to be doing well. They continued their negotiations with France, and for two years Edward was unable to conduct extensive military operations owing to the antagonism of his nobles and their rigid regard for the minimum obligation of feudal service.—Edward marched against Caerlaverock Castle, and took it, with all the heraldry, the pride and the glitter of chivalry behind him : but his chivalry insisted on going home after forty days in the field.—On representations from Philip of France a short truce was concluded at Dumfries in October, 1300, which lasted until May of the following year. Pope Boniface also intervened on behalf of Scotland, but after his own fashion, and his declaration that the realm of Scotland was held in fief of the Court of Rome, and that Edward had intruded to the disinheritance of the Church of Rome, did nothing to pacify the English king ; even his refractory barons resented the Papal admonition to 'remove his hand,' and united with Edward to assert, and to inform His Holiness, that 'the sovereignty of Scotland belonged to the regality of England.' Edward again invaded Scotland, but in January, 1302, in a triangular treaty with France and Scotland, he consented to a truce of ten months' duration.

Shortly after this the Bruce was in friendly communication with Edward, and in April he re-entered the King's peace.

III

WHY, after all his efforts on behalf of Scotland, did the Bruce now forsake his own country and reassert his allegiance to Edward? Because the Comyns were growing too strong; because the Scottish cause appeared to be triumphing—' all the country was rising because the English officers had no troops to ride upon them '; and because a Scottish triumph, at that time, would have meant the triumph of Balliol or the Comyns, and the eclipse of the Bruces.

As one of the Guardians, Bruce had nominally held Scotland for Balliol; and it is not impossible that for some months he was more concerned with the freedom of Scotland than with the person of its king. But the claims of his own family cannot have been immaterial to him for any length of time. He believed in his family's right to the throne, as did many other people, and he had good cause for his belief. When, therefore, it became apparent that owing to the crescent influence of the Comyns Scotland's cause was Balliol's cause and theirs, Bruce abandoned Scotland and took service again with Edward.

What did he hope to gain by this move? He did not mean to retire from active politics and settle down on his English estates. Had he, then, coldly determined to help Edward stamp out the strength of the Comyns, and of all their adherents and friends in Scotland, so that his own way to the throne might be clear—and then, having made use of Edward, to turn against him and lead a new rebellion? Or did he hope that Edward would now recognise his right to the Scottish throne, and present it to him in return for service in the field? If Edward, in 1302, had offered to make Bruce King of Scotland on condition of his becoming Edward's man, would Bruce have accepted? Would he, as the price of kingship, have admitted that ' the sovereignty of Scotland belonged to the regality of England '? He might have done. Fortunately, however, he was saved from this temptation by Edward's determination to rule Scotland for himself.

The English king was a good argument for democracy. He has been applauded for his statesmanship : but his statesmanship was merely a desire to surround himself with conquered peoples. He has been praised for his chivalry ; and his chivalry, bright though it was with banners, commanded the three days' sack of Berwick, the murder of Wallace, and the brutal slaying of prisoners. Wantonly cruel in his youth, his old age nourished a savage obsession. ' This king,' says Fordun, ' stirred up war as soon as he had become a knight, and lashed the English with awful scourgings ; he troubled the whole world by his wickedness, and roused it by his cruelty.' His tomb displays the austere motto *Pactum serva* ; but he kept faith by personal interpretation of the nature of an oath, by imposing a time limit on his promises, by exercising a kingly right to legitimate falsehood when necessary. He prided himself on his love of justice ; but had he loved honesty more his justice might better have warranted his pride. His piety was ostentatious, his domestic life was unstained. Stubborn zeal for his own glory often gave him sufficient force of character to browbeat his testy and contumacious barons and compel them to fight unwanted wars for him. He was brave and determined : he could swear, ' By the blood of God, though all my fellow-soldiers and countrymen desert me, I will enter Acre with Fowin, the groom of my palfrey, and I will keep my word and my oath to the death ! ' Nobody but Fowin and the people of Acre could quarrel with the nobility of that assertion, but his equally violent determination to annex Scotland not only impoverished his own country but nearly ruined Scotland, and left, as a legacy to each, hatred for the other that lasted for centuries. For a hundred years there had been no serious antagonism—a little bickering, perhaps, but no major conflict—between England and Scotland. It was Edward's insensate desire for self-aggrandisement that bred the awful enmity between them. He was, moreover, a good soldier, and sufficiently open-minded to make use of his enemy's virtues : most of his English archers, for instance, were Welsh bowmen.

Against such a king only a truly united country could hope to stand—and in Scotland the sea-serpent is a more frequent visitor than unity. When Bruce deserted Scotland the Scottish cause was apparently lost, and the cause of Scotland-under-the-Comyns was really lost. The downfall of the Comyns and the Balliols also involved the final defeat of Wallace. But a compensating hope appeared for the cause of Scotland-under-the-Bruce.

At this time Bruce was certainly unmoved by the kind of patriotism that animated Wallace. That flaming spirit, with its dark core of hatred for England, its bright spearhead of passionate love of Scotland and love of freedom—freedom and Scotland one burning vision—was not yet the Bruce's spirit :

it was to be, but not yet. Bruce had large estates both in England and in Scotland—and it is easier for a camel to go through the eye of a needle than for a rich man to play William Wallace. Bruce was a politician, and if his present policy was to assist Edward in overthrowing the Comyns, to remain loyal to the English king so long as the English king was useful to him, and then, being by then the only serious claimant to the Scottish throne,[1] to claim it and lead Scotland in a new rebellion against Edward, or Edward's successor—if this were his policy, then he was long-headed, far-sighted, cool, determined, and unscrupulous. If, on the other hand, he hoped to be given the throne as a reward for diligence in Edward's service, and to occupy it as Edward's vassal, then he was merely an energetic fortune-hunter.

There is reason, however, to believe that his ambition was the former one, the major and more perilous one. In the first place he must have remembered Balliol's fate too well to hope for any great stability or satisfaction in ruling as Edward's tenant ; and in the second place there is the fact that on June 11, 1304, when he was high in Edward's favour, he came to a secret agreement with Bishop

---

[1] His father had retired from politics. In 1302 he was living in Norway. He died in 1304.

Lamberton by which they promised mutual assistance 'in view of future dangers.' Bruce was obviously preparing the ground for a *coup d'état*. Lamberton, a patriotic and resolute man, was tied neither to Bruce's party nor to the Comyns. He had been for long the supporter and friend of Wallace, and he was always a determined champion of the independence of the Scottish Church. He would not lightly have allied himself with one of Edward's nobles, and his name on the bond proves its significance.

It is equally clear that Bruce was planning far ahead, since the year 1304 was no time for rebellion. Edward, crossing the Border in 1303, had conquered Scotland far more thoroughly than in his triumphant foray of 1297. He had marched through the north country, from Perth to Aberdeen, to Elgin and Kinloss, and met with little opposition. Sir John Comyn surrendered to him at Strathord. The other leaders, all save two, came in to offer their submission and their allegiance. And all the castles of Scotland— save one—were in English hands. Stirling Castle, under Sir William Oliphant, held out for three months against a mighty siege-train, and, lonely now in their defiance, Wallace and Sir Simon Fraser were unrepentant still.

Stirling yielded at last, more to hunger than

to the *Lup-de-guerre* and the *Tout-le-monde*, the Robinet, the Parson, and the other cumbrous engines that pelted the rock with boulders and Greek fire ; and presently Wallace was the only foe unconquered or unallured. He was hunted with bitter hatred and vicious device ; for zeal in their pursuit of him the fallen leaders of Scotland were promised remission of their sentences of banishment ; and the nobles of Scotland joined in the chase, or made show of joining it.

Wallace was captured in July and executed, with savage circumstance, on August 23, 1305. He was no traitor to Edward, for he had never been in Edward's peace ; he was a prisoner of war, and his execution was judicial murder. In the sentence delivered against him Edward laid no claim to those ancient rights of dominion over Scotland of which he had previously made so much ; he relied simply on the claims of conquest : 'After our lord the King had conquered Scotland, forfeited Balliol, and subjugated all Scotsmen to his dominion as their king . . .' Wallace, then, was neither traitor nor rebel, but simply the rearguard of a beaten army.

The summer of his execution saw another change in the Bruce's fortunes. In 1304 he had been actively engaged in Edward's campaign, and had assisted in the supply of engines for the siege of Stirling ; he had succeeded to his father's estates and done homage for them ; and certain debts due to the Exchequer, inherited with the estates, were respited by Edward. In March, 1305, he attended a parliament at Westminster, and he was one of three Scots—the others were the Bishop of Glasgow and Sir John de Mowbray —whose opinion Edward solicited as to the proper place, time, and representation for a parliament that should concern itself with Scottish affairs ; and whose advice he requested as to measures of defence for Scotland. Having learnt their opinions, the King approved them ; and having received their advice he answered : ' And as to the defence of Scotland, let the same be entrusted to the *custodes* and ministers of the King, and to the *communitas* of Scotland, in such manner as the Bishop of Glasgow, the Earl of Carrick, and John de Mowbray shall consent and ordain.'

In the same month Bruce petitioned Edward for the forfeited Carrick estates of Sir Ingram de Umfraville ; and Edward granted his request. Thereafter Bruce returned to Scotland, and at the end of May the *communitas* met at Perth to elect its parliamentary representatives in accordance with the scheme of government drafted by Bruce, the Bishop, and de Mowbray.

In July Wallace was captured ; in August he was executed. Mark now the decline in Bruce's fortune.

In September a parliament met at Westminster to frame the Ordinance for the government of Scotland ; the Bruce was not a member. In October the Ordinance was promulgated ; no office, no share in Scotland's government, was found for Bruce ; but he was ordered to place Kildrummy Castle ' in the keeping of one for whom he shall answer '—a sinister command that indicated no confidence in him and little more in his nominee. On October 10, de Umfraville was reinstated in his lands in Carrick, which, six months earlier, had been given to Bruce. About the same time Edward instituted proceedings—but unsuccessfully—to recover from Bruce certain feudal debts alleged (the allegation was disproved) to have been contracted by the elder Bruce in 1277 and 1282. And on October 26, when four temporary Guardians were appointed for Scotland, Bruce, so lately the King's adviser, himself a former Guardian, was not one of them.

The change occurs, very strikingly, at the time of Wallace's death. Till then Bruce was steadily advancing on the road of preferment ; but apparently he came to a bridge, and the bridge broke. In the succeeding months

Edward revoked his favours and regarded Bruce with hostility and suspicion. Why? It has been suggested [1] that the occasion of the rupture was indeed Wallace's death ; that his capture not merely dated the rupture, but caused it.

Among the documents in Wallace's possession were certain 'confederations and ordinances made between him and the magnates of Scotland.' It is not impossible that the Bruce's name was found in one of these confederations—Bishop Lamberton, with whom Bruce had made a secret agreement in 1304, had for long been Wallace's close friend and ally—for though Wallace had always been Balliol's man, Balliol was now an exile in France, and his chief supporters, the Comyns, were no longer regarded as leaders or potential leaders : Wallace, then, seeing (with Lamberton's eyes to help him) Scotland's only hope in Bruce, might well have promised to help him in his fight for the throne. If any such bond, or anything implying the existence of such an understanding, had indeed been discovered, then the sudden change in Edward's behaviour is wholly explicable.

But whatever the reason for it, the fact is clear : Bruce was out of favour and a suspect person. And early in 1306 he substantiated

[1] Barron.

44

Edward's suspicion in a rash and foolish way.

On February 10 he met the Red Comyn in the church of the Minorite Friars at Dumfries, and there killed him. This unfortunate occurrence has been embroidered with a variety of stories : it is said, on the one hand, that Comyn had betrayed the Bruce's plans to Edward, that the Bruce had escaped from England in a sudden romantic way, and, meeting Comyn in Dumfries, promptly assaulted him ; another story is told—with a full reporting of private conversations—of an elaborate plot, conceived by Bruce and his brothers, to murder the Comyn in cold blood ; while Barbour magnifies the killing into a general brawl in which many lost their lives. But the first story is invalidated by the fact that Bruce, not being in England, had no need to escape from it ; the second is disproved by the untimeliness of the killing, which clearly shows it was done, not in cold blood, but in quick unthinking heat ; and Barbour's magnification of the episode is irrelevant, for though twenty others had been killed, their death would not have increased the gravity of the crisis that the Comyn's death precipitated.

Bruce was now committed to premature declaration of his intentions. His plans were incomplete, the time was not yet ripe for rebellion. Edward was growing old, but Edward was still alive. Bruce, beyond question, had meant to wait for news of Edward's death before raising his standard. That would have been the proper time for him to claim the throne of Scotland and lead its people into another war of independence ; for the Prince of Wales had neither his father's resolution, nor skill in war, nor love of war. But many years of ill-feeling, the heritage of his blood, and a last flame of temper had undone the Bruce's careful policy : the Red Comyn was that Comyn who had ' leaped ' upon him in the Council in Selkirk Forest, whose family had been for long a barrier to his ambition, and now, perhaps, now when his new plans were maturing and he sought the Comyn's alliance, the Comyn refused, threatened to betray his plans, or boasted of having already betrayed them : their argument grew heated, a spark fell on old dry tinder, anger flared beyond control—and Comyn fell before the high altar with Bruce's sacrilegious dagger in his side.

Promptly the Bruce atoned for his folly and his sin by a display of admirable resolution. Henceforward he made no mistakes and never faltered. He protested no repentance for the Comyn's death, he sought no means of craving Edward's forgiveness, but with clear understanding of its perils he accepted the situation in which he found himself and boldly displayed the royal colours which had been so prematurely uncased.

His friends and confederates, though few in number, were fortunately true. The Bishop of Glasgow gave him absolution, and coronation robes from the episcopal chest. At Scone, the ancient capital, the Celtic capital, he was crowned King of Scots, and Isabella, sister of the Earl of Fife and Countess of Buchan—whose husband was a Comyn and his enemy—claimed the right of her family to put the crown on his head. There were present at the coronation the Bishops of St. Andrews, Glasgow, and Moray, and the Abbot of Scone : the Church was with him, and those princes of the Church are not least among the heroic names of Scotland. His four brothers, Edward, Nigel, Thomas, and Alexander were there. The Earl of Lennox, the Earl of Athol, Gilbert de la Haye and his brother Hugh, David Barclay of Cairns, Alexander Fraser, Walter de Somerville of Carnwath, David of Inchmartin, Robert Boyd, and Robert Fleming were others who shared the dedication of that defiant ceremony. There were also present the King's nephew, Thomas Randolph, afterwards Earl of Moray, and young James Douglas.

IV

EDWARD appointed Aymer de Valence his lieutenant and commander of the forces in Scotland, and daily messengers from the fierce old king rode northwards bearing letters urging him to more feverish activity against the rebels and to new oppression. A proclamation was issued that all who were in arms against England were to be pursued and taken, dead or alive, and those who did not aid in the pursuit were to forfeit their estates and be imprisoned. All who had a share in Comyn's death were to be drawn and hanged. All who were taken in arms against King Edward, and all who gave shelter to them, were to be hanged or beheaded. Bruce's estates in England—in Durham, in Middlesex, and elsewhere— were immediately declared forfeit ; his castle of Lochmaben, his lands of Annandale, were given to the Earl of Hereford ; and his earldom of Carrick was bestowed on Henry de Percy. Hurriedly an army was mustered, its command given to Prince Edward, whom the King knighted along with three hundred

48

others, and the avenging force, glittering with so many new spurs, rode to justify them on the insurgent Scots.

Meanwhile Robert gathered what friends he could, and found most of them in the Church, in his own country of Galloway, and north of the Highland line.—A certain cardinal, visiting England on a diplomatic mission, on hearing of Comyn's death had ' donned his pontificals, denounced the murderers of the said Sir John as excommunicate, anathematized, and sacrilegious, together with all their abettors, and any who offered them counsel or favour ; and expelled them from Holy Mother Church.' [1] But the stouthearted bishops of Scotland defended Robert's cause, and preaching friars declared a holy war.—By the end of June the Scottish king was in command of a useful army : he had ' all the force of Scotland which was on his side, and some fierce young fellows easily roused against the English.' [2] He offered battle to de Valence, who was then in Perth, and de Valence declined the challenge. But the English refusal to fight was not cowardice, but strategy. A few hours later, when the Scots were off their guard and a third of their force was out foraging, de Valence attacked and routed them. Robert himself, fighting in

[1] Lanercost Chronicle.   [2] *Scalacronica.*

D   49

his shirt, narrowly escaped capture ; Randolph and many others were taken prisoner ; and the dark shadow of defeat fell on the patriots' cause.

The Bishop of Glasgow had been captured a few weeks earlier ; the Bishop of St. Andrews was taken a month later ; but the Bishop of Moray was still free and preaching to his people that ' they were not less deserving of merit who rebelled with Sir Robert to help him against the king of England and his men, than if they should fight in the Holy Land against pagans and Saracens.' Edward complained most bitterly to the Pope about this aspersion on his cause, and furiously commanded de Valence to capture the Bishop at all costs. The English king's well-known energy was now chiefly devoted to letter-writing ; his senile fury was not exhausted by endless repetition, and the ferocity of his commands showed no loss of strength, though their effect was somewhat impaired by monotony. A fair example of his style may be found in a letter containing instructions for suitable punitive measures to be taken against Sir Michael de Wemyss and Sir Gilbert de la Haye : ' Seeing that we have not found in Sir Michael good word or good service, and that he has now well shown himself to be such indeed, on which account we hold him a traitor and our enemy, we command you that ye cause his manor where we lay, and all his other manors, to be burnt, his lands and his goods to be laid waste, and his gardens to be stripped clean, so that nothing remains there, and all others such may take warning thereby. . . . And as to Sir Gilbert de la Haye, to whom we showed great courtesy when he was lately with us in London, and in whom we thought we could well trust, and whom we have now found to be a traitor and our enemy, we enjoin that ye cause all his manors and houses to be burnt, his lands and his goods to be destroyed, and all his gardens to be stripped, so that nothing remains, and that worse be done to him, if worse can be, than is aforesaid of Sir Michael.'

After his defeat at Methven King Robert took to the hills, and when privation drove him thence—

> ' the maist part off his menye
> Wes rewyn, and rent ; na schoyne thai had,
> Bot as thai thaim off hydys mad '—

he came to Aberdeen, where his brother Nigel, his Queen, and his daughter Marjorie met him, and other ladies joined their little force,

> ' That for leyle luff, and leawté,
> Wald partenerys off thair paynys be.'

The approach of de Valence drove them into the hills again, where, apparently, James

Douglas by his energy and skill in hunting and fishing was a great help to them and filled their moving larder with venison, salmon, trout, and such lesser delicacies as minnows and eels. They travelled westwards, and at Dalry in Argyll encountered John of Lorn, a bitter enemy, whose force was greater than theirs. There was a brisk fight, but Robert's miniature army was hopelessly outnumbered, and he ordered a retreat. He himself maintained a stirring rearguard action while his people withdrew into safety. Then he sent his Queen and the other ladies, who could no longer endure the hardships of forced marching, ambushes, and cold weather, to the castle of Kildrummy in Aberdeenshire under the escort of his brother Nigel and the Earl of Athol.

Having consigned them to this fancied security, Robert, with Douglas and a force of about two hundred men, continued his march to the West. They were all on foot now, for their horses had been required to mount the Queen's party, and in the high hills they were already aware of the approach of winter. Nor were the inhabitants more friendly than the season. The King therefore decided to make for Kintyre. Presently they came to the shore of Loch Lomond and found no boat but a little thing that would carry three men at a time.

To march round the loch would have taken them into John of Lorn's country, or Menteith's, who was equally hostile. So by infinite repetition of the journey they crossed in the little boat, and to pass the time King Robert—so Barbour says—told his men stories of the Twelve Peers of France. Soon after this they were fortunate enough, while foraging, to meet the loyalist Earl of Lennox, who was overjoyed by the encounter, for he had thought Robert was dead. Sir Nigel Campbell, whom Robert had sent in advance to procure shipping, was successful in his errand, and the royalist army embarked somewhere on the Clyde and sailed, or rowed, for Kintyre. Lennox, in the rear of the little fleet, had hard work to escape the galleys of John of Lorn, who promptly came in pursuit. In Dunaverty Castle, at the southern extremity of Kintyre, the King was hospitably received by Angus of the Isles. But his enemies were hunting him hard : by the third week in September Dunaverty was closely besieged, and Edward was hurrying forward reinforcements for the investing troops. They had come too late, however, for King Robert had quietly put to sea, and nearly five months passed before he showed himself again on the mainland of Scotland.

Edward, in the meantime, was richly feeding his large appetite for revenge. The Prince of

Wales, marching northwards through Scotland,
' took all castles with a strong hand. But they
hanged those who had taken part in the aforesaid conspiracy, most of whom they caused first
to be drawn at the heels of horses. . . . Among
those who were hanged were not only simple
country folk and laymen, but also knights and
clerics and prebendaries.' [1] He besieged and
took Kildrummy Castle, but the Queen and
her ladies had fled to the sanctuary of St.
Duthac's chapel at Tain. From there they
were removed by the Earl of Ross and given
into the custody of the English. By Edward's
orders the Queen, the Princess Marjorie, and
the Countess of Buchan were confined in cages
built into turrets in the castles of Berwick,
Roxburgh, and the Tower of London : but,
lest he be accused of barbarity, the cages were
furnished so as to resemble as far as possible
a *chambre cortoise*, and two female servants,
' advanced in years and not gay,' were
appointed to attend the Queen.

Nigel Bruce was captured at Kildrummy
and hanged at Berwick. A few months later,
Thomas and Alexander Bruce, landing with
some force at Lochryan, were defeated, captured, and taken to hear sentence from Edward
himself, who was then at the Priory of Lanercost
in Cumberland : by his command Alexander

[1] Lanercost Chronicle.

54

was hanged ; Thomas was drawn at the tails of horses through Carlisle, hanged, and afterwards beheaded. Sir Simon Fraser, captured a little while before the siege of Kildrummy, was executed in London : he suffered hanging, evisceration and the burning of his entrails, and decapitation. His head—trumpets sounding the while—was set upon London Bridge beside the weathered mask of Sir William Wallace. The Earl of Athol, captured at sea, suffered an identical fate, save that his gibbet was thirty feet higher than Fraser's and his head was set upon a loftier spike—for he was the King's cousin.

All winter Scotland lay licking her wounds, and when, early in the following year, Robert returned, it was to a land impoverished by the loss of his dearest friends, a sore and sorely troubled realm, a kingdom in which there was not an acre of ground that he could call his own.

V

BARBOUR says—and his statement has often been repeated—that Robert spent the winter of 1306 on the island of Rathlin, thirteen or fourteen miles south-west of Kintyre and four miles from the north coast of Ireland. It is, however, quite impossible to believe this. The English intelligence service was remarkably efficient, and Rathlin, an island only six miles long, was part of the lands of Bisset of the Glens of Antrim, one of Edward's adherents : that Robert and his party, small though it may have been, contrived to lie hidden there for more than four months, their presence known only to the islanders, puts an unwarrantable strain upon even the most accommodating credulity.

Neither Fordun nor Gray,[1] moreover, so much as mention Rathlin ; the Lanercost Chronicle says that the Scottish king was 'lurking in a remote island,' which, written in Cumberland, is a poor description of Rathlin ; while Hemingburgh declares he

[1] *Scalacronica.*

had gone into 'the farthest isles.' Three
English chroniclers [1] say that he fled to Norway, and Norway would indeed have offered
friendly refuge, for the late king (the Maid's
father) had married, as his second wife,
Isabella, King Robert's sister. But Robert
returned to Scotland in the first weeks of 1307
—he was in Arran in February—and in the
fourteenth century January was not the usual
season in which to undertake a voyage from
Norway to the west coast of Scotland. If,
however, we so far extend the chronicler's
Norway as to include the Norwegian dominions,
the Orkneys or the Shetlands would very well
suit Hemingburgh's 'farthest isles' or the
'remote island' of the Lanercost Chronicle. It
is known, from one of Edward's letters, that
Robert's staunch supporter the Bishop of Moray
was in Orkney that winter ; it is on record that
Robert subsequently made a grant of £5 to
the cathedral of St. Magnus in Kirkwall ; and
an Orkney tradition asserts, not merely that
he wintered in those islands, but that his host
there was an udaller called Halcro, who later
fought with him at Bannockburn. The Orkney
tradition may therefore be accepted, and the
events of 1307, which in the absence of any
communication between Robert and the Bishop

[1] One in St. Albans ; Rastell, 1529 ; Fabyan, fifteenth
century.

57

can only be regarded as a happy coincidence, will be discovered as parts of a concerted plan.

In January Robert was ready to invade Carrick ; in February his brothers Thomas and Alexander landed in Lochryan with several hundred Irishmen ; and about the same time the indefatigable Bishop of Moray began to raise the North. This synchronisation of widely separated attacks was the strategy which had been used in the rising of 1297, and now, as then, the Highlands played an all-important part. In its beginnings, however, the campaign was not very successful. The Irish force was heavily defeated, and its leaders were captured and executed. Robert and Douglas, embarking on the wildest phase of their adventures, displayed a marvellous talent for remaining undefeated in face of desperate odds, for evading certain capture, and for snatching minor victories from an enemy of overwhelming strength. And the Bishop of Moray's pious endeavours during the early months of 1307 may be judged from a report written by the English officer commanding at Forfar on May 15 : according to his information, ' Sir Robert de Bruce never had the goodwill of his own followers or the people at large, or even half of them, so much with him as now ; and it now first appears that he has right, and God is openly for him, as he has destroyed all the king's power both among the English and the Scots, and the English force is in retreat to its own country, never to return. And they firmly believe by the encouragement of the false preachers who come from the host, that Sir Robert de Bruce will now have his will. . . . If Sir Robert can escape any way thither (that is, 'both beyond and on this side of the mountains'), or towards the parts of Ross, he will find them all ready at his will more entirely than ever, unless the king will be pleased to send more men-at-arms to these parts.'

Clearly the Bishop and his priests had not handicapped their patriotic sermons with too close adherence to the facts, for when this was written Robert had been successful in only a few minor enterprises. Five days earlier he had won the battle of Loudon Hill : it is possible that news of this had reached the English commander at Forfar, but there was certainly no time for the victory to have had repercussions in the Highlands. The Bishop had been doing some useful propaganda.

Robert, however, had much to do before he could find his way to the friendly North. The little island of Rathlin now claims an authentic place in history, for in January Robert landed there with a force of some three

hundred men, most of them recruited, pre-
sumably, from the Western Isles.[1] Their
presence was almost immediately reported to
Edward, who ordered Bisset of the Glens of
Antrim to join Sir John Menteith and Sir
Simon Montacute in order to 'put down
Robert de Bruce and destroy his retreat.'
Before this could be done, however, Douglas
had made a successful reconnaissance in
Arran, and Robert had joined him there.
He was now within striking range of Carrick,
and having sent a trusty man to investigate
the enemy's strength and disposition, and to
discover what chance there was of securing
reinforcements, he crossed the narrow sea by
night and landed near Turnberry.   The report
he received was dispiriting : the country
swarmed with English troops, Turnberry
Castle was strongly held by Henry de Percy,
and there was no hope of raising local support.   Nevertheless, it was decided to attack,
and before daybreak the little force stormed
the village below the castle, where many of
the garrison were billeted, and, waking them
with the sound of breaking doors, put them
to the sword.   The castle was too strong to be
taken, but Percy and his men were excessively
alarmed by the sudden invasion of their peace,
and remained within its walls.   Robert and

[1] Halcro, the Orkney udaller, is said to have given him 40.

his men withdrew with what booty they could find, and Percy, shaken by the surprise attack and ignorant of the invaders' strength, made no effort to retaliate.

His inactivity gave Robert time to look for recruits, but with the exception of forty men that a cousin brought him he was unsuccessful, for the people could not shake off their fear of the English. Had the Irish landing-party at Lochryan, under Thomas and Alexander Bruce, been successful, some part of the South-west might have risen, or Robert, joining hands with them, would have been in command of a force large enough to attempt some considerable exploit. But the Irish had encountered a Galloway army under Sir Dugald Macdowall, a bitter enemy of King Robert, and been cut to pieces. The Scottish cause lay in the doldrums.

Douglas took the opportunity to visit, with two companions only, his estates in Lanarkshire, where he perpetrated a picturesque outrage that captured people's attention, though its military significance was negligible. Coming with circumspection into Douglasdale, he found in Thomas Dickson, a man of substance, a loyal friend who secretly mustered a small company of sympathisers, and a plot was made to surprise the English garrison of the castle during their worship in St. Bride's chapel—Palm Sunday was conveniently near. The English soldiers, carrying their green branches, entered the church, and Douglas followed in a countryman's disguise. One of his supporters raised the battle-cry too hastily, and the English had time to adopt a defensive formation in the chancel. They offered a stout resistance, but the Scots, with Thomas Dickson first in the attack, over-powered them and killed the greater part. Then Douglas and his followers, returning to the castle, which was inadequately garrisoned by the cook and the porter, ate the dinner that had been prepared for English consumption, and kindled a fire whose abominable fumes made a pillar of smoke that was much regarded. It was useless to try to hold the castle, so having set aside the portable loot—weapons, clothing, and silver—Douglas ordered the remaining stores to be collected in the wine-cellar, and barbarously executing his prisoners threw their bodies into the foul mess of malt and meal and wine, and burnt the castle above them. This bonfire of groceries and murdered men was known as the Douglas Larder.

Meanwhile the English and their allies of Lorn and Galloway were building a human barricade round King Robert's retreat in the south-western hills. His hiding-place was somewhere in that wild and lovely triangle made by the lands of Carrick and Galloway. The hills of Galloway—to a Lowlander they are mountains—are like a segment of Highland scenery, mollified as regards rock and snow, but lovely and spacious, dignified by sufficient height, darkened or dressed in green by deep glens, and diversified by small lochs and forty tumbling streams. In the Bruce's time they were, in parts, heavily wooded ; for a mobile force, defending itself principally by evasion, the situation was perfect. Yet such was the strength of the forces encircling him that every move had to be made with the foresight and caution of chess-players in a masters' tournament, and the only hope of escape was the tiger's chance when his jungle is invaded and the beaters surround him : he must find the weakest part of the line and break it.

De Valence, Edward's commander-in-chief in Scotland, already held the northern slope of the hills, and John of Lorn with some men-at-arms and eight hundred Highlanders was hurrying to join him ; the seaports on the west were held by Percy ; Macdowall and his Galloway troops were on the south-west ; to the south, along the little river Cree that flows out of Loch Trool, were Sir Robert de Clifford and his men ; and to the east, in

Nithsdale, was the Warden, Sir John de Botetourte, with seventy horsemen and two hundred archers. When the circle was complete, Sir Geoffrey de Mowbray, like a ferret to bolt the coneys, went in with three hundred Northumberland bowmen to search the fastnesses of Glentrool.

It was this move, perhaps, that drove Robert northwards, and by bringing him into contact with de Valence and John of Lorn's Highlanders set afoot an adventure that Barbour describes with some detail. Robert, whom Douglas had now rejoined, had not more than four hundred men : in front of him was de Valence with a superior force, and behind him, or almost behind, was John of Lorn, who had made a circling movement under cover of rising ground. To fight against such odds would have been stark folly, and simple flight would have brought instant pursuit. Robert therefore complicated his withdrawal by splitting his force into three parts, and, having named a rendezvous, ordered each detachment to conduct its own retreat. John of Lorn, however, had with him a potent ally, a bloodhound that used to belong to Robert, and with its help he was soon in hot pursuit of the King. Robert again divided his force, but the hound, making no mistake, still held after him. Then he ordered the handful that

64

remained with him to scatter, and with a single comrade, whom Barbour calls his foster-brother, continued his desperate flight in full view of the pursuit. Five Highlanders, fleeter of foot than their fellows, were ordered to course him, and unhappily for themselves soon ran him down : the King at bay was danger-ous : four he killed himself, and his foster-brother accounted for the fifth.

But the pursuit, with the hound in leash, was closer now. The King and his men took cover in a wood, and there Robert, wearied by the chase and the fight, came near to owning defeat, and said he could go no farther. But his foster-brother, a gallant fellow, urged him on, and being unable to outrun the pack they used a little guile. For there was a stream in the wood, and they took to the water, and when the hound came to the stream it was at fault. And having cast in vain, up and down, John of Lorn philosophically declared :

> ' We haiff tynt this trawaill.
> To pass forthyr may nocht awaile.
> For the woid is bath braid and wid,
> And he is weill fer by this tid.
> Tharfor is gud we turn agayn,
> And waist no mar trawaill in wayne.'

Or, says Barbour, there is another tale, for some declare that the King's man was a skilful archer who turned back at peril of his life and shot the hound.   But whichever story is true, he continues, it was at the stream in the wood that Robert baffled the pursuit and made good his escape.

It is impossible to discover from Barbour's narrative either the precise sequence of events or the progressive movement of forces during this period of desperate hide-and-seek.   He describes, however, some stirring adventures that the King survived, and he establishes the fact that Robert possessed, in addition to mental gifts, the primitive quality of kingcraft : the ability, that is, to overcome his opponents by personal strength and an individual aptitude for war.   There is, for instance, the story of the traitor whom de Umfraville hired to assassinate him : early one morning, having retired to some bushes out of sight of his men, Robert was surprised by the would-be murderer and his two sons : the King had no one with him but a page, who carried a bow and an arrow —and the King had his sword : the traitors were challenged and would not halt : Robert took the bow and shot the eldest of them through the eye : the sons, one armed with sword and axe, the other with sword and spear, rushed on the King and fell, axeman first, spearman following, beneath his sword : and then with most royal regret, says Barbour, he pronounced their epicedium :

66

> ' Thai had bene worthi men all thre,
> Had thai nocht bene full of tresoun :
> Bot that maid thair confusioun.'

On another occasion the hunted King, alone, encountered a company of Galloway men at a ford, and slew fourteen of them. ' Strang wtrageouss curage he had,' says Barbour, and after judicious consideration of various kinds of bravery bestows his highest praise on ' hardyment that mellyt is with wyt ' ; nor can there be any doubt that in Robert this marriage of intellect and physical daring was most happily consummated. Barbour knew nothing of politics, nothing of strategy, little enough of tactics : but his tales of personal combat may well be accurate to a handstroke, and even the sententious conversation he reports may sometimes be very near the truth, for it is such things, words and the manner of a blow, that live clearly in simple memories, and Barbour talked with men who had known the King. It is useless to read him in the expectation of finding an orderly description of the patriots' campaign, but he will give you a sudden glimpse of the truth, the detail of a bypath adventure, that is easier to believe than to refute. After Robert's escape from John of Lorn and the bloodhound, for example, he tells how the King and his foster-brother met three of their enemies, one of them carrying a sheep on his shoulders, and how, in a state of poised hostility, action suspended but watchful as a leopard on its branch, they went to a deserted cabin, and killed the sheep, and roasted it, and ate.   And the King, having eaten heartily and being weary, slept.   And presently drowsiness descended also on his foster-brother, and

> ' he mycht nocht hald wp his ey,
>   Bot fell in slep, and rowtyt hey.'

Then the other three took their swords, and had not the King, roused by the snoring or the nearness of danger, waked instantly, there would have been the end of Scotland's hope. In the scuffle that followed the three were slain, and so was the poor foster-brother, who rose, not briskly like the King, but dizzy from slumber, and took his death-stroke as he stumbled to his feet.

Hot-foot after this escape, Barbour describes a night-foray against the English, and the killing of more sleep-drugged men.

This, then, was the manner of the second part of Robert's apprenticeship to sovereignty : he had played the politician, lordly and astute, balancing Edward's strength against the Comyns ; that phase was over ; and now he was using hand-to-hand and hand-to-mouth shifts like the youngest brother in a folk-story.

Presently de Valence made ready for a new offensive against the elusive King. He had temporarily withdrawn to Carlisle, leaving spies to inform him of Robert's movements, and now, having learnt that Robert had definitely established his headquarters in Glentrool, he hurriedly returned to Scotland with a strong force. He halted in a wood near Glentrool, and sent forward a female spy to discover the precise disposition of the Scots: despite his large superiority in numbers, de Valence's task was not simple, for the pass before him was too rough and narrow for cavalry, and Robert's position, being hard to attack, was correspondingly easy to defend; de Valence's hope lay in surprise, and his caution in first sending the woman to reconnoitre was ill-advised, for she betrayed him.

Without waiting for their spy to return, the English, under de Clifford and de Waus, advanced into the hills as far as a defile called the Steps of Trool. Robert, warned by the woman's loose tongue, was ready for them. There was a sudden alarm, a flight of arrows, a furious downhill charge, and the English, trapped by the hills, caught in loose formation on the steep shores of the loch, were thrown into hopeless confusion by the attack of a force whose numerical inferiority—Barbour says the English were fifteen hundred strong, the Scots three hundred—was compensated by its extreme mobility. The English were badly defeated, and de Valence again returned to England—so Barbour says—with great anger in his heart.

In his anger one may readily believe, but if he crossed the Border it was only to recross it immediately, for late in April he was in Bothwell Castle on the Clyde, prosecuting the war with undiminished vigour.

Robert had now begun campaigning on a larger scale. His little victory in Glentrool had given him a chance to leave the hills, and his success in defying, eluding, and defeating de Valence, having wakened hope again in the South-west, was bringing him recruits. He marched into the lowlands of Ayrshire, where his sovereignty was dubiously acknowledged, and continued his progress northwards to Cunninghame. De Valence suffered another reverse when a detached force under de Mowbray, proceeding against Robert in Ayrshire, was ambushed and defeated by Douglas. Then, if Barbour is to be trusted, de Valence again fell into a rage, and admitting his ineptitude in guerilla warfare issued a formal challenge to Robert to meet him in battle under Loudon Hill on the tenth day of May. But it matters little whether or not the challenge was actually uttered : the battle took place. Nor would such a challenge be surprising—in formal battle de Valence had every prospect of success—but that Robert was willing to risk his little army and meet the English in open field is indeed astonishing. The little army must have grown. His recruiting march through Ayrshire had clearly been a successful one. And clearly he had gained confidence in his men, and they had confidence in themselves and him.

Robert, choosing a position between two peat-mosses, strengthened it by digging trenches that would guard his flanks from cavalry. Barbour estimates his strength at six hundred fighting-men and as many ' rangale '—ill-armed, undisciplined supporters, that is : the English, he says, were three thousand strong, which is certainly an exaggeration. But though they were no more than a third of that, they had the advantage of heavy cavalry, mail-clad knights on covered horses, enough to make a handsome spectacle as they rode to the attack. It was a mass of light and colour that moved towards the trenches. Chivalry clad itself in gay hues. De Valence's shield of blue and white bars, on which sat ten little red birds the shape of doves, had shields as cheerfully painted on either side of it. So glittering an army—helmets burning in the sun, hauberks

71

' white as flowers,' bright spears, gay pennons, and multi-coloured shields—so shining a troop they were they looked the angels of heaven's host, says Barbour.

But the Scottish pikes had no respect for a handsome appearance, and the Scottish position was strong. Before nightfall the English were defeated and de Valence was in full flight for the castle of Ayr. Three days later Robert discomfited another English force under Sir Ralph de Monthermer, who also fell back upon Ayr. Then Robert, following up his victories like a good general, laid siege to Ayr, but was compelled to raise the siege when English reinforcements—de Valence's army, re-formed, and counter-attacking, per-haps—threatened his position. So strong was the new English offensive that Robert was forced to seek his old retreat in the hill-country of Galloway, and for the next couple of months he was again on the defensive. The English forces and their allies in the South-west, roused by a succession of small defeats, took once more the upper hand. De Valence re-inforced the garrison and strengthened the castle of Ayr ; led punitive expeditions into Carrick and Glentrool ; and vigorously searched the hills. In face of this offensive the Scottish king, biding his time, waited for time to help him.

72

Time helped him nobly, and in early summer King Edward died. From October of the previous year to the spring of 1307 Edward had been at Lanercost in Cumberland, old and sick and fretting for vengeance. When the days grew longer his strength, for a little while, returned. He was dissatisfied with de Valence's conduct of the war in Scotland, and he resolved to cross the Border himself. He sent to London for his tents, and on Whit Sunday reviewed his troops. Four hundred horsemen, decked with green leaves, rode past him, and the old King was well pleased with the display and grew merry to see his fine soldiers again. He gave his travelling-litter to Carlisle Cathedral, a thank-offering, and rode northwards. But he had outlived his strength. Dysentery attacked him again, and on June 7, at Burgh-on-Sands, he died, being sixty-eight years old. His *idée fixe* was not diminished by the approach of death : he bade the Prince of Wales send his heart to the Holy Land with an escort of a hundred knights, but carry his bones from place to place, wherever he should march against the Scots, unburied till his ancient enemy were utterly subdued. Edward II, however, declined this unpleasant legacy, and having taken his father's body to York, handed it over to the Archbishop for burial in Westminster Abbey.

The new King of England then returned to Carlisle and crossed the Border early in August at the head of a magnificent army. He advanced as far as Cumnock in Ayrshire, where he remained for two or three weeks. But his appearance was more warlike than his intentions, and on August 25, very peaceably, he led his army home again, having accomplished nothing.

No sooner had he gone than the Scots raided Sir Dugald Macdowall's lands in Galloway. They wrought such destruction that the Earl of Richmond, now Lieutenant in Scotland in de Valence's place, was hurriedly ordered to go to their defence with all the strength at his disposal.—Sir Dugald's lands were largely garrisoned by English troops.—It is not certain that Robert himself accompanied this punitive expedition against the man who, six months before, had sent his brothers to their death. The strategic centre of the war was no longer in Carrick or Galloway. At last the time had come for him to go northwards, to consolidate his strength in the Highlands, and perhaps he set out for Inverness immediately after Edward had started his retreat to England. If he waited to revenge himself on Macdowall first, he can have waited only till his raiders got their teeth into Galloway, and then he must have travelled north at speed : for by

Christmas he had two more victories to his credit, one secured by negotiation, the other by frontal attack. He took with him his brother Edward, the Earl of Lennox, Sir Gilbert de la Haye, and Sir Robert Boyd ; and he left Douglas as his lieutenant in the South-west.

Douglas celebrated his new command with another brisk dramatic exploit : he recaptured his castle in Douglasdale, that had been re-built since the burning of the Larder, by means of a second ruse. Having concealed a sufficient force in the neighbourhood of the castle, he tempted the garrison by sending forward four-teen men, disguised in country frocks, who led horses laden with fodder. The castle gates opened and the garrison happily came out to commandeer the hay of which their stables were badly in need. Then the fourteen countrymen threw off their bundles of hay and mounted their horses : Douglas and his men came out of their ambush : and the castle garrison, attacked in front and rear, was quickly defeated. The castle was again de-molished, but this time, more merciful than he had been, Douglas spared the lives of his captives and set them free. The Constable, however, a valiant and amorous young man called Sir John de Wanton, was killed, and on his body was found a letter from his lady

in which she promised to love him if he
proved himself by holding for a year

> ' The awenturus castell off Douglas,
>   That to kepe sa peralus was.'

—Happy Wanton, who in the one path could
serve both love and his king, and, being doubly
defeated, has been remembered for his double
gallantry !

VI

EDWARD II was ' not industrious, neither was he beloved by the great men ; albeit he was liberal in giving, and amiable far beyond measure towards those whom he loved, and exceedingly sociable with his intimates. Also in person he was one of the most powerful men in his realm.' [1] He was assuredly a more amiable person than his predecessor, but as a reigning monarch he was ill-equipped for the fourteenth century. During the old King's lifetime he had regularly been forced to attend his father's campaigns in Scotland, and the glittering prizes of a military career had been scrutinised, enumerated, and extolled, for his benefit, with such hot earnestness, such prolixity, that he had grown weary of their tedious dazzle. As soon as he became his own master he avoided unnecessary warfare and no longer pretended even to find pleasure in the dust and bruises of a tournament. He enjoyed simpler amusements, and more elegant amusements. On his travels he was accompanied

[1] *Scalacronica.*

by Genoese fiddlers and a lion, and he was interested in such primitive drama as the times afforded. Having signalised his release from paternal discipline by leading his army out of Scotland, he celebrated it by recalling from exile Piers Gaveston, in whose company he delighted, as he did in the company of grooms and boat-men. In addition to the exotic entertainment afforded by lions, Italian music, and Gaveston, he found relaxation in such simple pursuits as ditching, thatching, breeding hounds, and work-ing in a smithy. The great men of the kingdom —by whom he was not beloved—showed an equal lack of sympathy for all his pursuits : and, of course, had he chosen to pursue the war against Scotland with a zeal equal to his father's, they would have intrigued against him, and bickered with him, and endeavoured to minimise their feudal obligations as stub-bornly as they intrigued against and bickered with Edward I. The nobles of England, who were fundamentally self-seeking and found no great profit in a Scottish campaign, were not fanatical enemies of Scotland ; nor were the people of England, who preferred peace to any war ; it was Edward I who had been Scotland's enemy, and who by his dominant self-will had been able to make his enmity effective. His death was therefore a major blessing to the Scottish cause.

It is true that on sundry occasions—notably in 1310 and in 1314—Edward II violently remembered his inherited claim to the Scottish throne and, with the occasional brief zeal of an easy-going man, undertook and commanded a new campaign against the ever-growing strength of King Robert. Once, it is true—in 1314—he moved against Scotland with all the force he could muster. But except for these periods of unusual energy the character of the war changed after 1307. Till then there had been a steady offensive, unremitting and remorseless, against every manifestation of Scotland's independent existence ; after 1307, with brief exceptions, England was on the defensive and the initiative passed to Robert, whose attack became unremitting and remorseless as Edward's had been. But to emphasise the comparatively static position of England under its new king is not to depreciate Robert's achievement. The English defensive position was enormously strong. In 1307 every Scottish castle of importance was still held by England or English partisans ; and in mediaeval warfare the castles were dominant factors. Robert was still a king without a kingdom, for in all Scotland there was no strip of land he could call his own, no walled town where his standard flew. He had survived the loneliest part of his struggle, he had won the little battles of Glentrool and Loudon Hill, he had gathered a small but gallant army, he had strong friends waiting his arrival in the North, and England's policy was no longer a forward policy : there is the sum of his credit balance. But against him were castles studding the land from Berwick to Inverness, strongly garrisoned, impregnable except to siege-train or starvation or Douglas's tactics ; and in the North, where his friends were, were also his enemies the Earl of Ross and John Comyn, Earl of Buchan.

Robert's strength in the North lay chiefly in the great province of Moray,[1] that separated, like a wedge, the northern earldoms of Ross and Sutherland from the north-eastern earldom of Buchan. Under their gallant young leader, Andrew de Moray, the men of that province had played a notable part when Wallace was the spear-head of Scotland's battle for independence ; the Bishop of Moray preached the same cause when the Bruce became its leader ; and now, as the English commander at Forfar had written,[2] the people were ' all ready at his will more entirely than ever.'

It is probable that the castle of Inverness had already been taken and destroyed when Robert arrived there after his raid on Galloway : the tasks that confronted him were

[1] Barron.   [2] pp. 58-59.

the subjugation of Ross and Buchan. Robert dealt first with the northern earldoms—Sutherland was temporarily under the influence of the Earl of Ross—and quelled their opposition by a very imposing display of strength. Ross was admitted to a six months' truce ; early in December he wrote to Edward II, apologising for his defection, and explaining that Robert had come with an army of three thousand men—the majority must have been Morayshire men—who, at the Earl's expense, quartered themselves on the marches of Ross and Sutherland, while Robert threatened to lay waste all his territories unless he made peace with him till Pentecost next, June 1, 1308. The Earl afterwards became one of Robert's faithful adherents, and his son Walter fought and was killed at Bannockburn.

Having brought Ross to terms, Robert turned to Buchan. Here his difficulties were greater. The Comyns were still the most powerful family in Scotland, and the blood feud between them and the King made quite untenable any hope of friendly or diplomatic agreement.—'The Earl of Buchan desires, more than anything else, to take vengeance of you, Sir King, for the sake of Sir John the Comyn that was slain in Dumfries,' says Barbour. And the King replies : 'I had great cause to slay him.'—Therefore to fight and to beat them decisively was Robert's only chance of securing himself against their otherwise constant menace. He marched to Inverurie, prepared to give battle. There, however, he fell seriously ill, and a great sadness took the heart out of his men. 'There was none in that company,' says Barbour, ' who would have been half so sorry to see his brother dead before him as he was for the King's sickness : for all their hope lay in him.' But Edward Bruce, Robert's brother, rallied them, and for greater security they carried the King, in a litter, to Slivoch, sixteen miles north-west of Inverurie.

New of their whereabouts and of the King's illness reached Buchan, who promptly advanced against them in strength. He was accompanied by Sir John de Mowbray and Sir David de Brechin. Apparently the King's army had dwindled to a fraction of its former strength—it would have been tempting Providence as well as the Earl of Ross to leave Moray unguarded—for Barbour declares that Buchan's following was as two to one. The King's men, however, found so strong a position in front of a wood that Buchan hesitated to attack. He sent forward his archers to worry the royalist force, and Edward Bruce replied by throwing out his own archers to form a defensive screen. For three days there was sniping between the rival bowmen, but there was no hand-to-hand fighting. This gingerly battle took place ' after the Martinmas, when snow had covered all the land.' The inclemency of the weather, doubly unkind to the defending army, was aggravated by lack of provisions, and after three days the royalists were threatened by starvation. They found security in audacity, and, bearing the King's litter in their midst, marched off in close formation in the very face of the enemy. And so bold was their front that Buchan dared not attack, though his army had steadily been growing in numbers during the three days of competitive archery.

The magnificent effrontery of this movement can be safely ascribed to Edward Bruce, whose talent for war consisted largely of reckless determination and belief in the efficacy of rapid movement ; and the fact that he withdrew his force in safety suggests that it was well armed and well disciplined : that is to say, that it still consisted of the small company (Lennox, de la Haye, Boyd, and their people) who had accompanied Robert from Galloway, together with certain gentlemen of Morayshire and their immediate followers ; it was an army, not an assembly of rustic loyalists.

Having marched to Strathbogie, and stayed some little time there, the King returned to

Inverurie and went into winter quarters.
Barbour says his army then numbered nearly
seven hundred men, and

> ' thai wald ly in to the plaine
> The wynter sesone ; for wictaile
> In till the plane mycht thaim nocht faile ' :

but unless Inverurie and the neighbouring
country were well-disposed to Robert—despite
the shadow of Buchan upon them—the problem of feeding so large a force must have
been difficult. Buchan, however, did not
leave them long at peace. He gathered a
' full great company ' and advanced as far
as Old Meldrum. On Christmas Eve, in the
morning, his lieutenant, Sir David de Brechin,
made an armed reconnaissance and near Inverurie cut to pieces an outlying party of royalists.
When Robert heard of this he rose from his
sick-bed and, disregarding all protests, prepared to lead an immediate counter-attack.
' Their boast has made me hale and sound,'
he said, ' for no medicine would so soon have
cured me as they have done.'

This swift offensive took Buchan by surprise.
His outposts, however, warned him of the
King's approach ' with banners waving to
the wind,' and he had time to order his
battle and station his camp-followers in support. His men made a goodly show, says
Barbour. But Buchan, who had already

shown his unsoldierly quality at Slivoch, now revealed entire lack of leadership. The King advanced in determined fashion : Buchan's line wavered : Robert pressed his attack harder : Buchan's front line began to give ground : then his supports, seeing their masters falter, turned and fled : the panic spread forward, the knights turned tail, the battle became a pursuit, and the beaten army was chased as far as Fyvie, where there was a castle with an English garrison. Some time later Edward Bruce is said to have conclusively beaten the Earl near Old Deer.

Robert now proceeded systematically to destroy the power of the Comyns. Barbour says that he

> ' gert his men bryn all Bowchane
> Fra end till end, and sparyt nane ;
> And heryit thaim on sic maner
> That eftre that, weile fyfty yer,
> Men menyt " the Herschip of Bowchane." '

But there was more in the Herschip than setting fire to crops and cottages and driving cattle ; and there was more than personal vengeance in it. The Comyns held the castles of Kinedar, Slains, Rattray, Dundarg, and Kelly ; their allies held three others ; and there were English garrisons in Aberdeen, Aboyne, Fyvie, and Kintore : all these strongholds had to be reduced before Robert could safely leave the North-east corner behind him and turn to other tasks of conquest, pacification, and consolidation. No general can afford to leave an unconquered enemy in his rear, and the Comyns were enemies of peculiar danger. They were strong, they were implacable, they represented the Scottish opposition to Robert ; their survival meant the persistence of internecine warfare, their destruction meant the reinforcement of Robert's prestige, the rallying to his standard of prudent sitters-on-the-fence and well-wishers whom fear of the Comyns had previously immobilised. The Herschip, in all its ruthlessness, was justified by necessity. Its strategic value was obvious—especially if we include the destruction of the castles—and its moral effect was tremendous.

In June the defeated Earl was appointed Edward's Warden of Galloway : he must have fled his own country not later than March. In July the citizens of Aberdeen joined King Robert in his successful assault upon the castle of Aberdeen. Before autumn every castle in Aberdeenshire and the country north and west of it had been captured save one : Banff was still held for England.

VII

A SWIFT campaign in Argyll; the subjugation
of Galloway; and ceaseless war against the
castles, the strong-walled outposts of England
—these were the tasks that now confronted
Robert.

The Macdowalls of Argyll and Lorn were
kin to the Comyns: Alexander of Argyll was
the Red Comyn's uncle. Alexander was an
old man, however, and the enmity of his son,
John of Lorn, was the principal menace to
Robert in the West. Having temporarily
pacified that part of Scotland north of Inverness; having destroyed all opposition in
Aberdeenshire; and the loyalty of Moray
being assured, the conquest of the West—the
scotching of John of Lorn, that is—was clearly
the next step in Robert's process of consolidation, and he essayed it, apparently, very
soon after the reduction of Buchan. July,
1308, is the probable date of his marching
against Argyll. His army was large, and
he was accompanied by Douglas, who had
recently come north with an important

87

prisoner, Thomas Randolph, the King's nephew: John of Lorn, after being defeated, said that Robert's army numbered between ten and fifteen thousand, figures which, though they cannot be taken as a serious estimate, may be regarded as a tribute to the imposing appearance of the royal forces.

The size of the advancing army made its progress comparatively slow, and John of Lorn had time to place an ambush in the Pass of Brandir, a narrow defile that gives access to the south-east shore of Loch Etive—a sea-loch —from the north-west shore of Loch Awe. The north-east wall of the Pass rises to the abrupt magnificence of Ben Cruachan. John of Lorn had his galleys in Loch Etive, and himself lay in one of them to wait the result of the battle—a result disastrous for him. His ambush was dislodged from above, and his Highlanders were defeated on their own ground. Douglas led the King's archers over the top of Ben Cruachan, and from the heights looked down on Lorn's ambush: the main army entered the Pass and was assailed from both sides: the men of Lorn shot arrows and trundled boulders down the slopes: but the King's men were lightly armed and light of foot themselves, and he promptly ordered a heather-stepping uphill attack that spoilt the enemy's defensive scheme: then Douglas,

88

heralding his approach by a storm of arrows, led a downhill charge, and though the men of Lorn offered sturdy resistance the two-sided attack defeated them, and presently they broke and fled through the Pass. From his galleys John of Lorn was able to see their headlong flight.

Shortly after this victory, and having seized a great wealth of cattle, Robert besieged and captured the castle of Dunstaffnage, the chief seat of the Macdowalls. Barbour says that Alexander of Argyll submitted and was received into the King's peace, but that John of Lorn fled seaward with his galleys and escaped. In March of the following year, writing to Edward II, Lorn complained that the barons of Argyll had given him no help in this campaign, and that Robert had attacked him both by land and sea : this means that Angus Og and the men of Kintyre were again active on the King's behalf. The power of the Argylls was broken ; presently they both retired to England ; Alexander died in 1310, and John of Lorn became Edward's Admiral of the Western Seas. Alexander of the Isles, an ally and a kinsman of Lorn, was captured and his lands were given to Angus Og, his brother, but Robert's faithful friend and one of his earliest adherents. The barons of Argyll, who had refused their help to John of Lorn, proclaimed their allegiance to the King, and under Angus Og the strength of the Isles was secured.

After his settlement of the West, Robert marched north to conclude his negotiations with the Earl of Ross, who in November or December of the preceding year had agreed to a six months' truce. Since that time Robert's position had grown very much stronger : he had destroyed the power of Buchan and pacified the West : his star was plainly rising. His new prestige had its proper effect upon Ross, who, at Auldearn in Moray, on October 31, 1308, made full surrender and tendered his homage to the King. Robert accepted his surrender with a liberal gesture : he not only established Ross in all his former lands and tenements, but granted to him the additional lands of Dingwall and Ferncrosky, and in return for this wise generosity, 'I, William,' said the Earl, 'for myself, my heirs, and all my men, to the said lord my King have made homage freely and have sworn on the evangel of God.'

Following the pacification of the North and the West, the conquest of Galloway was completed in the early months of 1309, after a prolonged struggle. After Buchan's defeat Edward Bruce, with Douglas, Lindsay, and Boyd, had been ordered south : on June 29,

1308, Edward Bruce defeated de Umfraville and the men of Galloway somewhere in the valley of the Cree, and forced him to retire to the castle of Buittle ; by piecemeal conquest and the capture of small castles Edward slowly continued the pacification of Galloway ; and before autumn, Douglas, campaigning in the Forest of Selkirk, captured Thomas Randolph, the King's nephew, who, after assisting at Robert's coronation, had been taken prisoner by the English, had fought most vigorously on their side and eagerly chevied Robert during his hide-and-seek days in Glentrool, and later was to rival Douglas himself in his daring exploits for the Scottish cause.

Barbour says that Douglas, coming one night to a house on the Water of Lyne, listened at the door and heard some one inside exclaim : 'The devil !' Whereupon, naturally enough,

> ' he persawyt weill
> That thai war strang men, that thar
> That nycht tharin herbryd war.'

After a sturdy scuffle Randolph was made prisoner, and Douglas, as already recorded, took him north to the King ; where Randolph, in reply to Robert's suggestion that they might now be reconciled, hardily taunted Robert with pursuing his war against England 'with cowardy and with slycht' ; to which the

King replied with dignified composure and committed Randolph to safe keeping.

In November Edward Bruce took the castle of Rutherglen, and returned to Galloway to meet a new English attack. One of de Umfraville's colleagues, Sir John de St. John, had gone into England after Edward's victory on June 29, and there recruited a strong force and recrossed the Border, says Barbour, at the head of fifteen hundred men. Edward Bruce, finding himself in the neighbourhood of St. John's army, withdrew his infantry and rode forward with his cavalry division, which numbered fifty. One of them, Sir Alan de Cathcart, lived long enough to tell Barbour the story of the reckless work that followed. —A heavy mist made visibility poor, but the little cavalry force discovered the line of St. John's march and followed him. Later in the morning the mist suddenly rose, and, less than a bowshot distant, Bruce saw the English army. Without hesitation he charged them and cut his way through. Then his gallant fifty re-formed, charged again, and again broke through the English ranks. Seeing their enemy dismayed and standing in confusion, Bruce led another charge, but the English did not wait for his third onslaught. They scattered and fled, and the large remnant of the fifteen hundred took to their heels before the mad gallantry of Bruce and his fifty horsemen.

> ' It wes a rycht fayr poynt perfay,'

says Barbour with some complacency ; it was certainly an exploit that perfectly illustrates Edward Bruce's genius for audacity. He was in truth

> ' a noble knycht ;
> And in blythnes suete and joly ;
> Bot he wes owtrageouss hardy,
> And of sa hey wndretaking,
> That he haid nevir yeit abaysing
> Off multitude of men.'

By the middle of March he was present at the parliament his brother assembled in St. Andrews. This parliament is interesting on three counts : its purpose, its constitution, and Robert's ability to convene it in St. Andrews.

Its chief purpose was to consider negotiations with France that had already been initiated, and to intimate to King Philip that Robert was now recognised as King of Scots by the nobility, Church, and *communitas* of the kingdom. Diplomatic conversations had been proceeding between Philip's envoys and the English Court to ascertain the possibility of a truce between England and Scotland, but though Edward II was not averse from pacific measures he was not prepared to admit Robert's title to the

Scottish throne, and the conversations were finally unproductive. Philip's diplomacy was revealed in the directions on the various documents in possession of the French mission : those meant to be shown in England were addressed to Robert de Bruce, Earl of Carrick, and those intended for Scottish eyes were addressed to the King of Scotland.

The names of those who attended the parliament are interesting because they indicate the areas on which Robert had so far depended for assistance. In addition to ' the barons of the whole of Argyll and Innisgall,' there are twenty-eight names recorded. Eight of these are southern names : Edward Bruce, Thomas Randolph, Douglas, James the Steward, Robert de Keith, Edward de Keith, Alexander de Lindsay, and Robert Boyd. The remaining twenty represent northern families : Scotland north of the Forth and Clyde was clearly the dominant factor in the earlier part of the War of Independence.

And, thirdly, the fact that Robert was able to summon his parliament to St. Andrews shows that by March, 1309, he had securely established his position in Fife. Brechin Castle had fallen to him ; Forfar had been captured ; and now Cupar had evidently been taken, and Fife acknowledged his sovereignty. These conquests were effected by surprise attack and ceaseless vigilance that pounced on opportunity like a seagull on galley-scraps : Forfar had been captured by escalade under cover of night, and though the manner of Cupar's taking is not known, Sir Thomas Gray, the author of *Scalacronica*, relates a couple of adventures that befell its warden—his father, a daring and skilful soldier whose service was full of gallant deeds and romantic accidents—which clearly reveal the nature of the Scottish offensive : an imaginative persistency in attack and constant emulation of the edacious quality of Time were its most notable characteristics.

By the summer of 1309 the only castles north of the Forth and Clyde still held for Edward were Banff, Dundee, and Perth : these were regularly reprovisioned and reinforced from English ships. Stirling was also in English hands. Perth and Stirling were so strong that their capture presented almost insuperable difficulties.

VIII

THE proposals for peace which the St. Andrews parliament had discussed received intermittent attention during the summer of 1309. Lacking the truly questing pacifism of doves, however, these overtures rather resembled homing pigeons : they could do no more than carry unacceptable conditions and return with a diplomatic negative. What negotiation failed to effect was secured by Edward II's devotion to Piers Gaveston, and by the Scottish climate : in the autumn of 1309 Edward despatched troops to Berwick and Carlisle, but their commanders were more concerned with their King's infatuated regard for his Gascon favourite than with prosecution of the war, and they agreed to a truce with the Scots : this truce, originally intended to expire on January 14, 1310, was subsequently extended for a material reason, for, says the Lanercost Chronicle, ' the English do not willingly enter Scotland to wage war before summer, chiefly because earlier in the year they find no food for their horses.'

During this interval of peace Edward reinforced his garrisons in Scotland, and the Scottish clergy, meeting in Dundee, asserted with martial emphasis their allegiance to King Robert. After a résumé of events antecedent to his coronation they declared that ' being no longer able to bear so many and so great heavy losses of things and persons more bitter than death, often happening for want of a captain and a faithful leader, with Divine Sanction we agreed upon the said Lord Robert, the King who now is . . . With the concurrence and consent of the said people he was chosen to be king, and with him the faithful people of the kingdom will live and die as with one who, possessing the right of blood and endowed with other cardinal virtues, is fitted to rule and worthy of the name of King and the honour of the kingdom, since, by the grace of the Saviour, by repelling injustice he has by the sword restored the realm thus deformed and ruined, as many former princes and kings of the Scots had by the sword restored, acquired, and held the said kingdom when often ruined in times bygone. . . . We, therefore, the Bishops, Abbots, Priors, and the rest of the Clergy, acting under no compulsion, have made due fealty to our said Lord Robert, and we publicly declare that the same ought to be rendered to him and his heirs by our successors forever.'

The ancient Church of Scotland, indeed, when threatened by English discipline and patronage, ever translated their duty to God in terms of praiseworthy loyalty to Scotland— a translation with which the God of Jacob could have no smallest quarrel—and to the noblest of secular causes revealed a devotion commensurate with that of the Early Christians to a faith more explicitly spiritual. Bishop Lamberton, that wise and gallant prelate, was still active in diplomatic negotiations for the welfare of his country ; abbots and preaching friars had supported Robert in peril of their lives, and still supported him in peril of their souls, in defiance of his excommunication by the Pope ; and Glasgow's heroic bishop, blind now, lay in an English prison waiting for the victory at Bannockburn to release him.

In the summer of 1310 Edward prepared a major offensive against Scotland, and in his preliminary arrangements showed both energy and acumen. He assembled a large fleet, and by the despatch of ships and men to Perth made of that all-important outpost a base of operations in the very heart of the enemy's country. In anticipation of success the Earl of Ulster—Robert's brother-in-law—was given power to receive the vanquished or the malcontent to Edward's peace, and in August

Edward himself reached Berwick with his invading army. But it was a smaller muster than he had ordered, and less loyal than he had hoped. His barons served unwillingly or not at all. They sent small and grudging contingents, and their contingents were late in arriving. At Berwick Edward was involved in another quarrel with the nobles, and he did not cross the Border till September. His hope of forcing a decisive battle was unrealised, for Robert wisely employed guerilla tactics and contented himself with harrying the outposts of a force too large for him to destroy. Edward, after marching as far north as Linlithgow, retired to Berwick and prepared to winter there. Seeing him in retreat, Robert followed him and did much damage in Lothian, which was in Edward's peace. Edward recrossed the Border, again seeking battle, but Robert again evaded him and created a useful diversion by preparing, or at least threatening, an attack on the Isle of Man : for this marine flanking movement he relied, presumably, on Angus Og and the galleys of the Western Isles. Then Edward began to weary of so stern a task as the subjugation of Scotland, and renewed negotiations for peace. Robert was not unwilling to respond, but presently he was warned that the English meant treachery, whereupon he terminated the peace conference by moving into Galloway and threatening the western march of England. Edward replied by sending Gaveston to Perth with two hundred men-at-arms to hinder the advance of any reinforcements that Robert might order from the North.

Gaveston remained in Perth till April, 1311, when he returned to Berwick. In July, in London, a melancholy duty confronted Edward : he was forced to preside over a parliament whose business was to pass sentence of perpetual banishment on Gaveston. His love for the undesirable Gascon had brought England to the verge of civil war. Gaveston, ' orgulous and supercilious in debate,' had in addition to graver faults a juvenile gift for labelling his enemies with derisive nicknames : de Valence, a swarthy man, he christened Joseph the Jew, and he offended the Earl of Warwick by calling him the Black Dog of Arden. This addition of pinpricks to the wasting disease occasioned by his influence over Edward made the barons implacable against him : but Edward's infatuation was hardly to be moved even by so nearly irresistible a force.

This political-economic-sentimental *impasse* was Robert's opportunity. He, ' having collected a large army, invaded England by the

Solway on Thursday before the Feast of the Assumption of the Glorious Virgin [August 12], and burnt all the land of the Lord of Gillsland, and the town of Haltwhistle and a great part of Tynedale, and after eight days returned into Scotland, taking with him a very large booty in cattle. But he killed few men besides those who offered resistance.' [1] Having brought back the cattle, he returned to England by way of the eastern border and marched as far as Corbridge, 'burning the district and destroying everything, and causing more men to be killed than on the former occasion.' [1] He laid waste those parts of Tynedale which he had previously spared, and after harrying for fifteen days returned to Scotland, the wardens of the eastern march being powerless to hinder him. The result of this brisk invasion was that Northumberland sued for a separate peace, and after negotiations paid £2000 for a truce till February 2, 1312. Certain parts of Lothian were also persuaded to buy peace till the same date. The war having become a war of aggression, Robert was now making it pay its expenses.

The Lanercost Chronicler—who, having the dubious advantage of living close to the Border while these events were taking place, knew what he was writing about—remarks at this

[1] Lanercost Chronicle.

point that ' in all these aforesaid campaigns the Scots were so divided among themselves that sometimes the father was on the Scottish side and the son on the English, and vice versa ; yea, even the same individual might be first with one party and then with another. But all those who were with the English were merely feigning, either because it was the stronger party, or in order to save the lands they possessed in England : for their hearts were always with their own people, although their persons might not be so.'

The tragedy of wealth has seldom been stated with greater force and simplicity. For most of the great landowners in the South of Scotland it was still a case of pull devil, pull baker—the irrational demon of patriotism plucking at their hearts, and the baker of security, of material welfare, tugging at their heels. Their estates were in danger, their conscience was perplexed. Happy were those like Douglas, landless and free, and their cousins in the North who had listened to their hearts first and believed the reckless friars who preached that ' they were not less deserving of merit who rebelled with Sir Robert to help him against the king of England and his men, than if they should fight in the Holy Land against pagans and Saracens ! '

Early in 1312, their marches being still

without adequate protection, Robert again
raided the north-eastern counties of England
and compelled them to pay for another truce.
Later in the year the strong castles of Dundee
and Ayr were captured for him. In the first
days of July a parliament was summoned to
Ayr, and Robert made public his intention—
or allowed it to become known, for it was
repeated to the English king—of sending his
brother Edward to invade England while he
himself invested the castles of Dumfries, Caerlaverock, and Buittle, and supported his
besieging forces by raiding across the Border.
This plan—if it was correctly reported by
King Edward's correspondent—was subsequently improved : in the middle of August
Robert crossed the Border with his whole
army and lay for three days at Lanercost
Priory. From there he advanced to Corbridge,
and having plundered and laid waste the
neighbouring country he sent forward a
detached force under his brother Edward.
Edward's column took Chester-le-Street, continued its advance, and seized and sacked
the city of Durham. Having wasted the surrounding country, Edward established temporary headquarters at Chester-le-Street and
waited there while Douglas, continuing the
advance with the spear-head of the column,
advanced as far as Hartlepool, which he

sacked. With a large booty and many prisoners Douglas then retired northwards, rejoined Edward Bruce at Chester-le-Street, and with him fell back on the main force at Corbridge. As a result of this well-contrived and very alarming invasion the people of Durham begged for a truce, and agreed to pay £2000 for immunity from attack until June 24, 1313—a period of ten months—and at the same time promised the Scots free access through the bishopric lands whenever they desired to make a raid. Northumberland secured an extension of the truce, for the same period, for a like sum, and Cumberland and Westmorland bought temporary peace for a smaller amount—they could not find so much as £2000—and the loan of hostages. On their way home the Scots attempted to capture Carlisle, but were defeated with heavy casualties. Without wasting more time—he had, of course, no siege-train—Robert recrossed the Border and with Randolph and the Earl of Athol proceeded to Inverness, where he held a parliament in the last week of October. Edward Bruce and Douglas concluded their remarkable campaign by laying siege to the castles of Dumfries, Buittle, and Caerlaverock, which were all captured by the end of March, 1313.[1] Their abundant energy was also suffi-

[1] Fordun.

cient during this time to attempt by escalade the capture of Berwick : for this purpose they made ingenious rope-ladders that would hook on to the walls, and had not the loud barking of a dog betrayed their attempt they would probably have succeeded in taking the garrison by surprise : as it was, they had to retire and leave their ladders behind them, which the English hung on a pillory ' to put the Scots to shame.'

For the sweeping success of his invasion Robert was greatly indebted to the disintegrating personality of Piers Gaveston. In the early days of 1312, defying the parliamentary sentence of banishment, the Gascon had returned to England. The barons cut off the King's supplies. Edward and Gaveston fled northwards, and for subsistence plundered York and Newcastle. Gaveston was captured in June, and by order of the Earls of Lancaster and Warwick was beheaded on the high road near the town of Warwick. Edward continued his feud with the barons, and internecine dispute prevented them from paying much attention to the northern marches : in January 1312 Edward had again offered peace, but his terms were unacceptable, and the war continued.

While Edward Bruce and Douglas were busy with their siege of the south-western castles, Robert, having dismissed his parliament in Inverness, essayed the capture of Perth, a walled and moated town, heavily garrisoned : the garrison included a hundred and twenty mounted men, so its total strength must have been very large. The strategic value of Perth was enormous, and its defences were commensurate. For six weeks Robert laid siege to it without success, and then, in full view of the garrison, who mocked his going, he marched away with all his army. But during the investment he had made an accurate survey of the moat and walls and discovered that part of the moat was comparatively shallow. After a week's absence he returned to Perth, under cover of a dark night, having armed certain of his men with ladders in addition to their ordinary weapons. The town lay before them, dark and silent and unsuspecting. Robert, in full armour, carrying a ladder and a spear, was the first to lower himself into the moat : the water was neck-high, and cold, for the month was January. Hastily but in silence his men followed him : Robert was the second man to reach the top of the wall. A goodly number had climbed it before the alarm was given.— The mediaeval system of depending at night on paid watchmen, rather than on sentries, was a great help to surprise attacks.—The town

was still sleeping when the attack began.
Robert, reinforcing a daring assault with
prudence, kept a strong guard with him to
deal with organised resistance or counter-
attack. The rest of the invading force, split
into small parties, set off through the streets,
and the bewildered citizens, caught in their
beds or fleeing in their shirts, woke to a more
dreadful nightmare than any they could have
contrived in their dreams. There was no
massacre, however. Robert had given orders
that life was to be spared as far as possible :
the majority of those within the walls were of
the same blood as those who came from without, and except for some more valorous than
reasonable in their defence, and others who
were notorious enemies of Robert, few, it
seems, were killed.—Barbour says that Robert
was merciful to the townspeople ; the Lanercost Chronicler says that he let the English
garrison go free ; Fordun declares that known
traitors, English and Scots, were executed.—
One may reasonably infer that killing was
selective and judicious, not haphazard. But
there was widespread looting, and many
gallant invaders who had climbed the wall
in stark poverty were by sunrise richly clad,
with money in their new pockets and new
armour on their backs. Then the walls of
Perth were demolished, its towers were razed,

its moat was filled, houses were burnt or pulled down—

> ' He levyt nocht about that toun,
>   Tour standand, na stane, na wall,'

says Barbour, and the Lanercost Chronicler declares that Perth was utterly destroyed. Its strength had been too great, its strategic value too obvious, to leave anything that might tempt the English to counter-attack, recapture, and rebuild it.

Four months later, in May, that is, Robert invaded and captured the Isle of Man. His activity was unceasing, his genius for effective movement astonishing : the secret of the art of war, as he practised it, was significant mobility. Consider the record of ten months, from July, 1312, to May, 1313 : in July he had held his parliament at Ayr and made his plans for the invasion of England ; he had led his army across the western march and then eastwards to Corbridge ; from there he had sent Douglas and his brother Edward on swift offensives against Durham and Hartlepool ; returning to Scotland, he left Douglas and Edward in charge of operations on the Border and proceeded to Inverness, where he held another parliament ; this progress, that flattered his friendly relations with the North, enabled him to give personal attention to any difficulties that had arisen from Argyll to Buchan, from Sutherland to Aberdeen ; then, presumably with northern troops, he captured Perth, and returned to the South-west in time to receive, from his old enemy Sir Dugald Macdowall, the surrender of the castle of Dumfries ; and a few weeks later he invaded Man. He conquered Scotland by forced marches and ruled it from the saddle.

The Isle of Man was a Scottish possession by right of purchase from Norway, but actual tenure went backwards and forwards, between England and Scotland, like a shuttlecock. Robert now presented it to his nephew Randolph, whom, in generous recognition of his conversion, valour, and loyal service, he had recently created Earl of Moray. The island would have been an excellent base for commerce-raiding on the west coast of England, but unfortunately Randolph was unable to hold it : it was recaptured in 1314 by John of Lorn—Edward's Admiral of the Western Seas—and Randolph had great difficulty in regaining possession.

The truce with the northern counties of England having by this time expired, Robert made plans to cross the Border again. But his threatened invasion was averted by a timely bid for peace. The price offered was acceptable, and another truce was sold. The north of England was now guaranteed against attack till September, 1314.

The next phase in the war was the reduction of Lothian, which was still held for England. It was guarded by strong castles, its officials were English nominees, and the large majority of its leading families were still adherents of England. By 1313, however, the English tenure had grown very insecure, and the condition of the people was acutely unhappy. They were subject to spoliation by the Scots and by their own nervous garrisons, and south-eastern Scotland was in a state of barely suppressed anarchy. Its conquest for Robert was distinguished by three famous exploits : Douglas's capture of Roxburgh Castle, Randolph's capture of Edinburgh, and the taking of Linlithgow Peel by William Bunnock, a farmer.

Bunnock achieved fame in harvest-time. The garrison of Linlithgow Peel had bargained with him for a load of hay, and he brought them a load as dangerous as Ulysses' Wooden Horse, for in the middle of it were hidden eight armed men. Bunnock led his waggon across the drawbridge, halted it squarely in the gateway, cut the traces, and cut down the porter : out came the eight men, in came the near-lying ambush, and presently the Peel was captured.

On Shrove Tuesday in 1314 Douglas approached Roxburgh Castle on all-fours. He had sixty men with him, also on their hands and knees, and with black cloaks thrown over them they sufficiently resembled, in the difficult gloaming, a herd of cattle. They came to the castle walls and scaled them by means of rope-ladders, iron-runged and hooked. The garrison, merry-making on the eve of Lent, were dancing, singing, and 'other wayis playing,' when the harsh cry of 'Douglas! Douglas!' rang out—and most of them had no trouble in keeping their Lenten fast that year.

In the same month Randolph took Edinburgh Castle by assault, as daring and brilliant a piece of work as any in the whole war. He had in his company a man called William Francis, who, some years before, had served in the castle. Francis, a hot lover in his youth—let his name be set above Leander's, for his ardour was more useful—had acquired, during his service in the garrison, the habit of climbing down the Castle rock to visit a girl in the town below, returning thence by the same perilous route before morning. He offered to show Randolph the path he had so often taken, and Randolph, with thirty chosen men, followed him one dark night and came by the voluptuary's way to the castle wall, not without pain and fear, for the craig was high and hard to climb, and while they were resting half-roads up they were startled by the watch passing along the ramparts, one of whom, inopportunely joking, cried : ' Away ! I see you well ! ', and threw down a stone. Recovering from this alarm, the rock-climbers continued their dangerous ascent, and presently reached the wall. The alarm was quickly given and fierce hand-to-hand fighting took place. But at the same time an attack was delivered on the south gate,[1] and when the Constable fell, killed in the melly by the wall, the defence crumpled, and Randolph, as he well deserved to be, was master of the castle. Having taken it he demolished it, and having demolished it he marched towards Stirling, where a crisis was approaching that Edward Bruce had recklessly invited.

Edward Bruce, having laid siege to Stirling —it is not known on what date—had made a compact with de Mowbray, its Constable, by which the latter agreed to surrender it should no relief come before midsummer, 1314. This impolitic agreement was, of course, an open challenge to England : it would be incredible were it not that compacts in the age of chivalry were often impolitic, and that Edward Bruce was notorious for light-hearted

[1] Lanercost Chronicle.

recklessness. Robert's comment on the bargain, as reported by Barbour, is sensible enough to be authentic, though its moderation is remarkable : ' That wes unwisly doyn perfay ! ' He then points out the folly of giving the English king time in which to prepare his attack, who from his wide territories could muster an army far more numerous than Scotland's defence : the Scottish cause has wantonly been put in danger. But Edward takes the wind out of his reproof by stoutly declaring that though all the English come, and more than all, ' We sall fecht all ! ' Whereat Robert ' prisyt him in hys hart gretumly.'

The English chroniclers say that Edward Bruce did not attack Stirling till after the fall of Edinburgh, and that Edward II's campaign for its relief was consequently hurried. It is known, however, that Edward had begun to make warlike preparations before news of the capture of Edinburgh could have reached him : the English chroniclers may have been a little inclined to post-date the challenge, as Barbour, who ascribes it to the summer of 1313, was surely guilty of ante-dating it. But whatever its date, the compact was made, and Stirling was Edward's goal when he invaded Scotland.

Once again he showed unusual and com-

mendable energy, and circumstances favoured
him more than they had in 1310. In reaction
against the murder of Gaveston the majority
of the barons were, for a little while, loyally
disposed towards their king, and Edward,
stirred by the Scottish challenge, summoned
a feudal muster without waiting to obtain
the consent of his parliament. Eight hundred
and thirty earls and barons, with their re-
tainers, responded to the summons—after some
delay—and proceeded towards Scotland.

On March 24 Edward summoned 21,500
infantry from Wales, the north of England,
and the Midlands. Four thousand archers
and other infantry were also ordered from
Ireland. Mobilisation proceeded slowly, however. The common people have never been
greatly interested in glory, and were it not
for knights in armour who could fight in
reasonable safety—and press-gangs—and commanders who comfortably direct a battle from
the rear—it is doubtful whether England or
any other country would ever have achieved
any glory at all : the world might have sat
under its fig-trees and sung the songs of
peace : and historians in the hollow lotus-
land have sickened with hope deferred of
battles that were never fought. We are inclined to think of the Middle Ages as martial
ages, but Edward I and Edward II seldom

114

succeeded in raising half the numbers specified in their mobilisation orders. Even with Bannockburn in the offing the English were strangely slow to grasp the forelock of glory and join their king on his great adventure. On May 27 Edward issued third writs of summons in which he peremptorily declared : ' We had ordered the men to be ready by a date already past. The enemy is striving to assemble great numbers of foot in strong and marshy places which it is very difficult for the cavalry to reach. Therefore you are to exasperate and hurry up and compel the men to come.'

This command was more liberally obeyed, and early in June Edward was in command of a very imposing army : ' Six or seven days before the Feast of St. John he left Berwick with more than 2000 armed horse and a very numerous infantry. There were enough men there to march through the whole of Scotland, and some thought that if all Scotland were collected together it could not resist the King's army. The multitude of carts stretched out in a line would have taken up twenty miles. The King, in his confidence, hastened day by day towards his goal. Short time was allowed for sleep, shorter for meals.' [1]

The English army took the inland route

[1] *Scalacronica.*

115

to Edinburgh, up Lauderdale and by Soutra Hill. The Scots made no attempt to harass it as it crossed the moors. They were waiting for it at Bannockburn. On Saturday, June 22, Barbour says the English marched from Edinburgh to Falkirk, full twenty miles. This was fine marching but poor preparation for a battle.

IX

BARBOUR, poet and patriot, but no statistician, declares that Edward's army was 100,000 strong : the microscopic eye of more recent historians has reduced the figure to something between 14,000 and 20,000.[1] Barbour says that the Scottish army numbered 30,000 : modern research elects a figure between 4000 and 7000.[1] To accept figures within the modern limits—but inclining to the upper, for the scholar's searching after truth afflicts him with a kind of ascetic incredulity, a diminution for virtue's sake, as the old historians, for glory's sake, affected a magnanimity of belief that led to a fabulous exaggeration—to accept a rough estimate of 18,000 Englishmen and 6000 Scots is reasonable and will clarify the sequence of events at Bannockburn : it is impossible to imagine armies of greater size—or of much greater size—executing the manœuvres ascribed to them, and in the limited space at their disposal there was hardly room for a more numerous battle.

[1] Ramsay and Mackenzie.

The English army included between 2000 and 2500 heavy cavalry [1] : fully-armoured soldiers on covered horses, that is ; the Scottish cavalry were light cavalry and numbered 500.

But disparity in numbers, either of cavalry or total strength, was not the most important difference between the two armies : the English army was a feudal army, the Scottish army a national army. Military science was decadent in England : armoured knights on horseback were still regarded as dominant figures in war and the most important members of an army, though experience had shown— at Courtrai in 1302, at Falkirk and Stirling Bridge—that pikemen in close formation were more than a match for cavalry unsupported by archers. A schiltron of pikes had, however, no defence against arrows. Now the English, having conquered Wales, where at this time bowmen chiefly grew, could put in the field several thousand archers of excellent quality ; but they could not use them properly because of the jealousy of the knights. Feudal cavalry, brave though they might be, were wretched soldiers : emulous of honour, without discipline, undrilled in tactics, they looked at war through the slits in their own helmets and were eager to outshine their comrades rather than the enemy. Sometimes

[1] Morris.

for a gesture they lost their lives : more often they simply lost their battles.

The Scots, on the other hand, had been well drilled by adversity and the genius of King Robert. They had, in 1314, no heavy cavalry. Poverty had saved them from that disability, for a charger able to carry horse-armour and an armoured rider might cost as much as £100, which at present values would be enough to buy a small aeroplane. Their army being an infantry army, they naturally put a proper value on infantry. Wallace had taught them to use a close formation—the schiltron—and receive cavalry on their pikes : he had drilled them in defence. King Robert, brilliantly improving Wallace's tactics, made the schiltron mobile ; it therefore became an offensive as well as a defensive formation. A steady advance in close order, carrying long pikes and facing fire, is far from easy : the Scottish drill must have been first-rate : but the Scots had this advantage, that gentle and semple fought side by side, and their section-leaders and right-hand men were their hereditary chiefs. The mobile schiltron was the tactical weapon that made Bannockburn a Scottish victory, as it was King Robert's preliminary strategy that prepared the way to victory.

The English army was advancing against Stirling from the south-east. It had a choice of two approaches to the Castle : one through the New Park, the other on level but marshy ground nearer to the Forth.

In the neighbourhood of Stirling the Forth, as if reluctant to come to the sea, meanders to the east with wide looping and relooping. Some three miles from the Castle it receives the Bannock, a burn that writhes and wriggles in its course as though even more reluctant to meet the Forth than the Forth is to meet the sea. The low-lying land between the Bannock and the Forth is known as the Carse : it was there that the main battle took place— the second day's battle, that is, for the first day was occupied with minor engagements on higher ground, at the entrance to the New Park, south-west of the Carse, and on the low north-eastern flank of the New Park. The Park was then somewhat thickly wooded. It rises in grassy slopes to a few modest heights : Coxet Hill is two hundred feet above sea-level, Gillies Hill is three hundred. The Carse, on the other hand, was distinguished even at midsummer by marshy pools, and towards high water the mouth of the Bannock received the influx of the tide.

King Robert first mustered his men in the Torwood, south of the Bannock. He anticipated an attempt by the English army to force its way through the Park, fronting which was a level plain suitable for cavalry. Having learnt that the English were approaching, he withdrew across the Bannock and prepared a useful defence against cavalry by digging small pits, close together and concealed by sticks and grass, in the flat ground at the entrance to the Park. His army, however, in four divisions, was so disposed as to guard both the approaches to the Castle, the high and the low ; Robert's division, guarding the Entry, faced south and the pitted plain ; behind him was Edward Bruce's division ; well behind that, by St. Ninian's Kirk, was Randolph, who fronted the Carse ; and Douglas, with a division nominally commanded by Walter the Steward, lay between Randolph and Edward Bruce. Randolph would lead the vanguard against a Carse attack ; Robert held the forward division in case of a frontal attack.

On the morning of Sunday, June 23, the army was in position. The men rose early, soon after sunrise, and Mass was celebrated. They would have no dinner that day, but bread and water only, for it was the vigil of St. John. Robert, having inspected and approved the newly-dug pits—that were to serve no purpose, however—issued a proclamation that any whose hearts were not resolute for victory and steadfast unto death should straightway leave the ranks ; and a general cry answered him that fear of death would keep none of them from fighting to the end. Then he sent the servants and ' small folk ' to find cover in a valley in the Park, probably between Coxet Hill and Gillies Hill.

Meanwhile Douglas and Sir Robert Keith had led a reconnaissance towards the English army, that on the previous night had reached Falkirk, ten miles from Stirling. They were deeply impressed by the magnificence of the invading host : burnished armour blossomed in the sun, flaming banners and bright pennons flaunted their colours above the dust ; basinets glinting in the morning light, shields ashimmer, and spear-heads winking, and the embroidered gaiety of knightly raiment ; the helmet and the helmet-feather burned like myriad flames above the endless host that marched against the ' few folk of ane sympill land.' Douglas and Keith galloped back to the King and delivered their report in private. Robert wisely forbade them to tell the men what they had seen, but issued instead a report that the English were advancing in disorder.

Three miles from Stirling Castle Edward was met by Sir Philip Mowbray, the Constable, who suggested that he should come no farther, as his advance might already be construed as a technical relief of the Castle. He also informed Edward that the Scots had blocked all the rides through the wooded Park. But Edward declined to halt. The English vanguard, commanded by the Earls of Gloucester and Hereford, pushed on in the direction of the Entry and Robert's division, while a regiment of cavalry, three hundred strong,[1] under Sir Robert Clifford and Henry de Beaumont, rapidly advanced by the Carse road. Their route lay directly beneath Randolph's division.

The Scottish leaders appear to have been watching the advance of Gloucester and Hereford so closely that Clifford's regiment was unobserved till it was well on its way into the Carse. Robert tersely informed Randolph that ' a rose of his chaplet was fallen.' Randolph made haste to cover his fault—it was a serious one, for Clifford had nearly turned his flank—and rejoining his men led them downhill against the English. His division consisted of five hundred spearmen. To lead them against heavy cavalry was none the less daring because it was a necessary move.

The English, however, might well have ignored the challenge, and ridden on to the Castle. That they accepted it is a tribute to their chivalry : they acknowledged the

[1] Barbour says 800.

obligations of their code and neglected their king's orders to pick up Randolph's defiance. Seeing the Scots advance, de Beaumont called to his men : ' Let us wait a little ; let them come on ; give them room ! '

Sir Thomas Gray, whose son wrote *Scalacronica*, was in the regiment. ' Sir,' he said, ' I doubt that whatever you give them now, too soon they will have all.' [1]

' Very well,' said de Beaumont, ' if you are afraid, be off ! '

' Sir,' said Sir Thomas, ' it is not from fear that I shall fly this day.' And he charged into the thick of the enemy, where he was fortunate enough to be taken prisoner, his horse having been killed on the pikes. Randolph's division had formed a hollow square, and the English horsemen attacked it in vain : it stood impregnable, like a porcupine between a couple of terriers : horses plunged helplessly against the pikes, and sometimes in a daring sortie a pikeman would leap from the ranks, point and withdraw, and return to his place in the bristling hedge. The English, raging in vain, threw spears and swords and maces at the enemy, and their weapons lay thick in the midst of the schiltron. Dust rose thickly round them, and from men and horses rose a sweaty

---

[1] This sententious observation suggests an access of wisdom after the event ; but it is piously recorded in *Scalacronica*.

steam, for the sun shone hotly and the fighting was desperately hard.

Looking down upon the fight it seemed to Douglas that Randolph was getting the worse of it. He sent a message to the King, craving permission to go to Randolph's assistance. Robert gave it, somewhat grudgingly, and Douglas ordered his division to advance. But when they came nearer they saw that the English attack was weakening, and Douglas halted his men lest he should rob Randolph of credit. The approach of Scottish reinforcements discouraged the English, who began to give way. Randolph pressed them hard and presently they broke and fled disorderly, some to the Castle, some back to their army. The Scots, weary after their long struggle, hot and most uncomfortably sweating, took off their helmets, wiped their streaming brows, and thanked God for victory. This affray took place beneath St. Ninian's Kirk.

Meanwhile King Robert had played a reckless part that would have better suited his brother Edward. The English vanguard, pressing forward, had come face to face with Robert's division. The English had advanced too rapidly and were not prepared to attack a position held in strength. Foremost of them was Sir Henry de Bohun, a kinsman of the Earl of Hereford. Perceiving the strength of the Scottish position, he turned his horse and signalled his people to retire. But at this moment the Scottish king rode towards him.

Robert, who had been dressing his ranks, was mounted on a little grey pony. He carried an axe, and above his basinet he wore a high crown. De Bohun recognised him and immediately accepted his challenge : a challenge that offered the English knight every advantage. With lance in rest, de Bohun charged. At the crucial moment Robert deftly swerved, and, rising in his stirrups as de Bohun thundered past, struck with his battle-axe—

> ' And he raucht till him sic a dynt,
>   That nothyr hat, nor helm, mycht stynt
>   The hewy dusche that he him gave,
>   That ner the heid till the harnys clave.'

This kingly smithy-stroke was the signal for a Scottish attack. Edward Bruce, bringing up his division in support, converted the impulsive forward movement into a general advance. The English vanguard, already inclined to retire and disheartened by the fall of de Bohun, turned in swift retreat. With a great shout the Scots quickened their attack, and some of the English were killed : but cavalry have great advantage in a retreat, and their casualties were few. The pursuit was soon abandoned, and the Scottish leaders, surrounding their king, reproached him for his foolhardy invitation to de Bohun : Robert, in a classical example of understatement, remarked that he had broken his battle-axe.

Soon after the discomfiture of the English van, Randolph appeared to report his defeat of Clifford's regiment, and the soldiers, doubly elated, pressed round to do him honour. For a while, it seems, discipline was forgotten, and the whole army came to see and applaud the man who had beaten mailed horsemen with a few hundred pikes. The King, however, was not unduly influenced by the prevailing excitement. He addressed his men, and after telling them how well they had done, and confessing his belief that so good a beginning should have a good ending, bade them decide whether to continue the battle or prudently retire. Their answer, natural in that exultant hour, was that they would fight. But Robert was seriously debating the wisdom of retiring to the wilder country of the Lennox, where natural obstacles would discount the numerical superiority of the English, should they follow, and where guerilla tactics might gradually destroy the invader without exposing the Scots to a major defeat. In view of Edward's overwhelming strength there was much to be said for such a plan.

Later in the day, however—or when the shallow dusk of midsummer had fallen—Sir Alexander Seton, a deserter from the English army, came in to the Scottish lines with valuable information. ' " Sire," he said to the King, " now is the time, if ever, to think of reconquering Scotland : the English have lost heart and are discouraged, and expect nothing but a sudden open attack." So he told him of their condition, and declared, upon his head and under pain of being hanged and drawn, that if he would charge upon them in the morning he would defeat them easily without loss to himself.' [1] Robert thereupon abandoned all thought of a strategic retreat and decided to give battle in the morning.

The English in the meantime were crossing the Bannock and making their camp in the Carse.[2] It was a wet uncomfortable place in which to pass the night, but they worked hard to bridge the burn and cover the pools with material from near-by houses—doors, thatch, and the like. It is said that some of the garrison from the Castle came down and helped them, bringing doors and shutters. They had little rest that night. So large an army would take long to cross the burn, and when they had crossed it and the small summer darkness fell, they were fearful of sudden attack. But though some were nervous, others were

[1] *Scalacronica* : the author's father being at this time a prisoner in the Scottish lines.
[2] Barbour and *Scalacronica*.

bitter because of the repulse of their vanguard and Clifford's defeat. The marshy triangle in which they lay, bounded on two sides by the Forth and the Bannock, had some defensive value as a camp ; but it was a poor battle-field, for its open side, towards the enemy, was so short that it gave the English no room to extend. By night a defensive position, by day the Carse might become a trap. It would be a trap if the Scots, attacking first and pressing their attack, succeeded in closing the triangle. But Edward and his advisers probably thought this impossible.

Again the Scots rose early, heard Mass, and frugally broke their fast. Robert, fully appre-hending the position, saw the English in their open trap, and immediately decided to close it. He forthwith ordered his advance. By his command the Scots had provided themselves with banners. Their dress and equipment were sober enough—spear and sword, basinet and leather coat, or jack and habergeon, and plated gloves—but the banners gave their advance a certain gaiety, and the men were in high fettle. They advanced in three divisions in echelon by the right—Douglas, Randolph, and Edward Bruce, Edward leading—and Robert followed in support.

Hastily and in some alarm the English mounted. Edward was amazed by the bold-

ness of the advance. ' What ! will yon Scots
fight ? ' he asked. ' Yea, surely,' answered
one of his knights, Sir Ingram de Umfraville,
who, being half a Scot himself, suggested
that Edward should order a retreat, when
the Scots, he said, being ever mindful of
plunder, would break their ranks and start
looting the English camp : and that, he suggested, would be a suitable opportunity for
counter-attacking. (Robert, indeed, after telling his men of the rich spoil that awaited
them, had warned them against the dangers
of untimely plundering.) But Edward refused
this suggestion : ' No one,' he said, ' shall say
that I avoided battle or withdrew from such
a rabble as that.'

When the Scots were quite near to the
English they knelt and repeated the Lord's
Prayer. ' They kneel to ask mercy,' said
Edward. ' But not of you,' answered Sir
Ingram ; ' yon men will win or die.' ' So be
it, then,' said Edward, and all his trumpets
sounded.[1]

Steadily the Scots advanced. Edward Bruce's
division, on the right, was the first to come into
action. Over against it lay the English van,
whose advance was delayed by a dispute
between Gloucester and Hereford as to who
should have the honour of leading it : when

[1] Barbour.

they encountered—armoured horse and pike-men—' and the great horses of the English dashed upon the Scottish spears as upon a dense forest, there arose a great and horrible din from the broken lances and the wounded horses, and so for a time they stood locked together.' [1]

Now Randolph's division came up on Edward Bruce's left, and Douglas came up on the left of Randolph. Opposed to them was the great mass of the English army, cavalry in front, infantry behind, and few of them with proper room to fight. They were caught in the trap. Some of the English archers, however, were well posted to the right and in front of the short English line. For a time they hindered the Scottish advance—a forward screen of Scottish archers was no match for them—but presently Robert ordered Keith's regiment of light horse against them, who promptly put them to flight. Robert was a masterly tactician : his cavalry, so few in numbers, were used in the proper place, at the proper time, and with admirable effect.

The din of battle grew louder as contact was made along the line. The smithy-sound of sword on helmet and spear against shield was mingled with the scream of wounded

[1] Barbour.

131

horses and the multitudinous susurration of straining lungs. There was no shouting, but the ring and the clatter of weapons, thudding blows, groans, and the clamour of fierce confusion. Robert, venturing all, threw his own division into the line, and the Scottish archers, rid of their opponents now, found what marks they could and played on the closely-packed host before them. The struggle was fierce and bloody and prolonged. Against the disciplined impetuosity of the Scots—twenty years of hatred in their blood, victory in their thoughts, and their movement all obedient to the King's drill—was opposed the huge unmanageable force of England, penned between the river and the burn, bravely fighting in front, desperate with inaction in the rear. Slowly the Scots pressed forward over ground slippery with blood, over gralloched horses and dying men. Edward Bruce had thrown back the English van, Douglas and Randolph were thrusting ever deeper into the armoured mass before them—Edward, Douglas, and Randolph, paladins of outrageous hardihood, of infinite skill and strength in arms—Douglas in a hundred fights kept his face unscarred—and Robert, blithe in battle, urged them ever to press on a little faster and a little faster.

Then the English began to weaken. The cry went up : ' They fail ! ' and the fiercer cry : ' On them ! on them ! ' Resistance slowly crumbled, and presently the flight began. Panic probably started in the rearmost ranks, that, as the front ranks fell back upon them, were still powerless to help.— Two hundred knights fled from the field who had never struck a blow. — Now came the famous irruption of the ' small folk,' the servants and yeomen who had lain in the valley behind Coxet Hill : curiosity seized them— they watched the battle—then impatience took them, and the infection of martial deeds, and hunger for action and for glory : they tied old clouts to spears and branches, and made banners for themselves, and fell in upon their elected markers, and with loud shouting came in haste to join the battle.

At the sight of this rude but numerous reserve the English lost heart entirely. They were already beaten, and now they acknowledged defeat. Their king, with de Valence and de Argentine at his reins, in the midst of a large company, broke past the left flank of the Scottish army, and fled towards the Castle. Edward, who went unwillingly, was nearly dragged from his horse, but manfully using a mace fought his way through. De Argentine, having seen that he was safe, gravely bade him farewell, and with heroic egotism returned to die : ' *Jeo nay pas este acoustome a fuyre, ne plus avaunt ne voil ieo faire.'*

King Edward was refused admittance to the Castle, whose Constable was ready to surrender it : he fled round the west side of the Park, closely pursued by Douglas and a small body of horse, but Edward's guard was too strong to be attacked, and reaching Dunbar in safety he escaped by sea. A swarm of English infantry, following their king, had gathered under the Castle crags. So many were they that Robert was compelled to hold his troops in check in case they re-formed and launched a new attack : this prevented the effective pursuit, and permitted the subsequent escape, of Edward and his bodyguard.

Looting and slaying, the ' small folk ' overran the battlefield. The English had marched with luxurious equipment : there was gold and silver plate to plunder, embroidered cloths, the armour of the dead, and armour that the living threw away so that they might run the faster. There was loot to the value of £200,000 [1] on the battlefield, and the many noble prisoners who were taken were worth noble ransoms. Scotland, winning a great victory, won also a great fortune at Bannockburn : mediaeval warfare, humaner than modern warfare, was also more equitable :

[1] About £3,000,000 in money of to-day.

Scotland, entitled to a large indemnity after twenty years of English occupation, had no need to sue for reparations, but collected them on the spot.

The pursuit of the English continued. The infantry who had gathered under the Castle crags were dislodged but not destroyed. They fled towards Berwick. A company of knights who sought safety in Bothwell Castle were received, and promptly betrayed by the Constable, Sir Walter Gilbertson. A mass of infantry, who had followed them, being refused shelter, continued their flight towards Carlisle. There seems to have been no great slaughter of the fugitives : loot, perhaps, assuaged the Scottish army's wrath. But England's battle casualties were high : anything from two hundred to seven hundred horsemen were killed, and how many infantry perished in battle, or were trodden to death in the flight across the burn, or were drowned in the Forth, is not known.

More than five hundred English knights and noblemen were held to ransom. The Earl of Hereford was exchanged for fifteen Scots who had lain long in English prisons : these included King Robert's wife, daughter, and sister, and the blind Bishop of Glasgow. Stirling Castle surrendered, and Sir Philip de Mowbray, its Constable, went into Scottish service. And now

' Robert de Bruce was commonly called King of Scotland by all men, because he had acquired Scotland by force of arms.' [1]

But to balance their immediate losses the English acquired tactical knowledge that, applied in later years, won for England the battles of Cressy, Poitiers, and Agincourt : they learnt to distrust their feudal cavalry and put more faith in archers.

[1] Lanercost Chronicle.

X

EVEN to the artist achievement without recognition is like a bed without pillows, and to the statesman it may be like a bed without a mattress. In statesmanship, indeed, achievement is hardly to be counted as such unless it has been accorded official acknowledgment. The king-maker and the nation-maker have scarcely fulfilled their purpose until the claims they make for their puppets and their peoples are recognised by neighbouring crowns and countries. Robert's task, therefore, was not yet complete. He had won Scotland by the sword and forged a sceptre in war, but until his sovereignty and the independence of his people were recognised in the councils of Rome and England, until that which existed in fact was acknowledged in writing above the signatures of the Pope and the English king, his work was unfinished. In the diplomatic conversations of 1309 a formula had been proposed which, had it been acceptable to both parties, would have brought peace : it was, quite simply, the recognition of Scotland's independence and Robert's sovereignty. But Edward refused to admit these allied facts, and the war went on. Bannockburn should have taught him and his barons the truth, but it did not. After Bannockburn Scotland was ready for peace and solicited peace : King Robert wrote to King Edward saying there was nothing he so earnestly desired as a permanent good-understanding between the two kingdoms : but the formula for peace was unchanged : and the rulers of England still refused to do business on such terms. Now and again England, or the northern parts of England, were forced to appeal for a truce. But for thirteen years there was no lasting peace. From time to time olive branches waved in the wind, but no fruit fell, and Robert discovered that the only way to get the olives was to beat the trees.

A few weeks after Bannockburn, Douglas and Edward Bruce were over the Border again, spoiling the northern counties ; and the history of the next thirteen years is a history of raid upon raid, of punishment implacably repeated until at last the English were driven to admit the obvious force of King Robert's claims and the manifest status of Scotland.

It is unnecessary to record in detail the repetition of hammer-strokes that Robert and

Douglas and Randolph dealt on the cringing counties beyond the Border. Year after year the Scots raided Northumberland and Cumberland, Durham and Yorkshire, carrying fire and sword as they went, cattle and the purchase-price of a new truce when they turned home again. They did not always come back unscathed, and though now they went openly as conquerors—no longer raiding with desperate audacity, but descending on the fold with the bold and peremptory air of Victory's favourites —victory did not always come to them at the first easy summons. They made a most determined attempt to capture Carlisle, Robert himself leading his troops, and despite their most furious attack and ingenious device, Carlisle refused to capitulate : Sir Andrew de Harcla, its Constable, was a gallant knight and a good soldier. They were beaten back from the walls of Berwick, and though on a later occasion they captured the town by assault, the castle yielded only to starvation. And the castle of Norham, commanded by the indefatigable Sir Thomas Gray, survived eleven years of constant peril and diversified a stubborn defence with romantic incidents such as the knight Marmion's adventure, who for love of a lady came there, as to the most dangerous place in Britain, to do battle against the Scots in a golden helmet, and went home a plainer and a wiser man, for the Scots, it is said, made shipwreck of his face—*ly naufrerent hu visage.*

There is indeed such a number of stirring episodes in the tale of these years that their more prosaic aspect of fear, starvation, and misery on the one hand, and stern policy on the other, is apt to be forgotten. Douglas laying his ambush among the birches by the Jed; Douglas's duel with de Neville, the Peacock of the North; the Bishop of Dunkeld throwing off priest's raiment—he wore armour beneath it—to rout the English invaders in Fife; Simon Spalding keeping watch on the walls of Berwick —these lively events rise like bubbles to the surface of the years, but underneath were poverty and plague and dread : underneath them was Robert's unyielding resolution to establish the independent sovereignty of Scotland beyond doubt or question, beyond legal quibble or the tortuous claims of politicians and land-hungry monarchs.

The remorseless punishing of the northern counties of England was his simplest weapon. In 1315 he essayed a more indirect move, a kind of knight's move, admirable in theory but less fortunate in practice. This was to send Edward Bruce to Ireland, as claimant to its throne, with a large army to support him in his adventure.

The Irish were already unhappy under English rule, which was indeed so far from being impartial that murder of a native Irishman was not considered a felony. Certain chieftains, notably the O'Neills of Ulster, having observed the successful campaign of the Scottish independents, now invited Edward Bruce to accept an Irish crown and help them against their oppressors. Edward accepted the offer and Robert provided him with an army. There was much to be said for this new campaign. In the first place, it enabled Robert to offer his brother a reward commensurate with his services in the Scottish wars; secondly, it gave Edward, a reckless and venturesome man, a congenial occupation; thirdly, it promised to establish a power friendly to Scotland on England's flank; fourthly, it struck immediately at Edward's strength in Ireland; fifthly, it would divert attention from Scotland and give Robert time to put his house in order; sixthly, it offered new glory to the Bruces—and the dynastic question had always been important to Robert; and lastly—but this tentatively, for the racial motif is not obvious—it would, if successful, lift the yoke from a Celtic sister-people.

For more than three years Edward Bruce fought for his elusive kingdom: on May 2, 1316, he was crowned, and on October 5, 1318, he was killed. For six months, from the autumn of 1316 to the spring of 1317, Robert himself was fighting in Ireland : there is a story that he halted his army outside Limerick for the sake of a washerwoman caught in child-birth, and rather than leave her behind delayed his homeward march till her baby was born : but this is a lonely item of mercy in the bloody history of the Irish campaign. Not only were Scots and Irish fighting against English and Irish, but the Irish fought among themselves, and famine joined war in horrible alliance. Randolph, who had accompanied Edward Bruce, twice returned to Scotland for re-inforcements. Victory and defeat came alter-nately, and Edward performed many brilliant exploits whose glory the surrounding misery tarnished. His Barmecide reign came to an end at Dundalk, as the result of his own reck-lessness. Refusing to wait for reinforcements that were only six miles away, he impatiently attacked an enemy far stronger than himself, and was killed :

> ' a noble knycht . . .
> Bot he wes owtrageouss hardy,
> And of sa hey wndretaking,
> That he haid nevir yeit abaysing
> Off multitude of men.'

His death necessitated a new Act of Succession. A parliament held in May, 1315, had declared that Robert's daughter, Marjorie, was the heir-apparent, but that—failing the birth of a son to Robert—she had agreed, in view of the special difficulties of the time, to be passed over in favour of Edward Bruce. Three years later Edward was dead, and Marjorie, married to the Steward of Scotland, had died in child-bed leaving a son. By an Act of 1318 this son was made heir to the crown unless Robert himself should leave male issue, and in the event of his minority Randolph was named his guardian. The same Act carefully defined the principle of succession, decreeing that succession should go first to the male issue of the Sovereign in their order of birth, next to the female issue, and, these being exhausted, to collaterals in the same fashion. Six years later, after twenty years of marriage—seven of which had been spent in prison in England—Robert's Queen bore him a son, David, to whom, when he was two years old, the clergy, nobility, and people took oaths of fidelity at Cambuskenneth in presence of their King; and it was decreed that, should David die without issue, the succession should go to Robert, the Princess Marjorie's son.

The King's scrupulous care in nominating heirs to the throne and defining the law of succession was largely dictated by his natural desire to establish succession in his own family

—dynastic motives had influenced him before patriotism moved him—but he also remembered the chaos of 1290, when there was a dearth of heirs and a glut of claimants, and these Acts were designed to prevent the recurrence of such disastrous confusion.

In 1317 the Papal Court again became actively interested in Scottish affairs. At Edward's instance the Pope issued a bull commanding, under pain of excommunication, a two years' truce between England and Scotland : it was addressed to ' our dearest son in Christ, the illustrious Edward, King of England, and our beloved son, the noble Robert de Bruce, acting as King of Scotland.' Two cardinals came to England with the bull, and the cardinals sent two messengers to Scotland :

' The King graciously received them and heard them with patient attention. After having consulted with his barons, he made answer, that he mightily desired to procure a good and perpetual peace, either by the mediation of the Cardinals, or by any other means. He allowed the open letters from the Pope, which recommended peace, to be read in his presence, and he listened to them with all due respect ; but he would not receive the sealed letters addressed to " Robert Bruce governing in Scotland." " Among my

barons," said he, " there are many of the
name of Robert Bruce, who share in the
government of Scotland ; these letters may
possibly be addressed to some one of them ;
but they are not addressed to me, who am
King of Scotland. I can receive no letters
which are not addressed to me under that
title, unless with the advice and approbation
of my parliament. I will forthwith assemble
my parliament, and with their advice return
my answer."

' The messengers attempted to apologise
for omission of the title of King ; they said
that Holy Church was not wont, during the
dependence of a controversy, to write or say
anything which might be interpreted as pre-
judicial to the claims of either of the contend-
ing parties. " Since, then," answered the
King, " my spiritual father and my holy
mother would not prejudice the cause of my
adversary by bestowing on me the appellation
of King during the dependence of the controversy, they ought not to have prejudiced my
cause by withdrawing that appellation from
me. I am in possession of the kingdom of
Scotland ; all my people call me King, and
foreign Princes address me under that title ;
but it seems that my parents are partial to
their English son. Had you presumed to
present letters with such an address to any

other sovereign Prince you might, perhaps, have been answered in a harsher style ; but I reverence you as messengers of the holy see." He delivered this sarcastical and resolute answer with a mild and pleasant countenance.

' The messenger next requested the King to command a temporary cessation of hostilities. " To that," replied the King, " I can never consent without the approbation of my parliament, especially while the English daily invade and spoil my people."

' The King's counsellors told the messengers that if the letters had been addressed to the King of Scots, the negotiations for peace would have instantly commenced. They imputed the slighting omission of the title of King to the intrigues of the English at the Papal Court, and they unguardedly hinted that they had this intelligence from Avignon.' [1]

Robert, who was busy with preparations for the siege of Berwick, continued work on his engines, unmoved by papal interference : ' I will listen to no bulls,' he said, ' until I am treated as King of Scotland and have made myself master of Berwick.'

When he heard of Robert's refusal to receive the bull, and of the way in which his messengers had been treated—for subsequently they were robbed of all their documents—

[1] *Foedera* : paraphrased by Hailes.

146

His Holiness was shocked and astounded, and his cardinals were ordered to excommunicate the Scottish king and all his adherents. The orthodox channels of excommunication were closed, however, as the patriotic clergy of Scotland declined to serve such hostile papers on their king, and the papal fulminations, echoing from beyond the Border, were strangely inoperative. Then the Papal Court grew angrier still, and more active. The excommunication was repeated, and papal denunciation, commination, invective and thunder-loud reproof continued to impugn the cause of Scotland. In 1319, moreover, when Edward II, roused by the fall of Berwick and momentarily at peace with his prime enemy the Earl of Lancaster, made large preparations to renew the war, the Archbishop of York was authorised by the Pope to advance him £2500 out of funds collected for a crusade.

The English attempted to recapture Berwick. Their army was large, their attack determined, and their equipment elaborate. Mobilisation orders for 8000 men were issued, ships were prepared to co-operate in the assault, and a monstrous movable engine called The Sow was constructed. The Scots, under Walter the Steward and with the assistance of a Flemish engineer called Crab, were equally determined and no less ingenious. But they were hard put to it to maintain their defence. Robert, however, created a diversion in their favour by sending Douglas and Randolph on a raid into Yorkshire. The English queen was then living in York : she escaped the raiders, but Yorkshire suffered severely at their hands : and the English clergy demonstrated their lack of martial skill : ' The citizens of York, without knowledge of the country people and led by my lord Archbishop William de Meltoun and my lord the Bishop of Ely, with a great number of priests and clerics, attacked the Scots one day after dinner near the town of Mytton, about twelve miles north of York ; but as men unskilled in war they marched all scattered through the fields and in no kind of array. When the Scots beheld men rushing to fight against them they formed up according to their custom in a single schiltron, and then uttered together a tremendous shout to terrify the English, who straightway began to take to their heels at the sound. Then the Scots, breaking up their schiltron, mounted their horses and pursued the English, killing both clergy and laymen, about 4000, and about 1000 were drowned in the water of Swale.' [1]

The Archbishop's plate and other furniture fell into the hands of the Scots, and the know-

[1] Lanercost Chronicle.

ledge that the Scots were successfully campaigning in his rear persuaded the English king to raise the siege of Berwick. Following these twin discomfitures the English sued for a truce, and for two years they were admitted to uneasy peace.

In January, 1320, the Pope summoned the Scottish king—not as the Scottish king, but as *nobilem virum, Robertum de Brus, regnum Scotiae gubernantem*—to attend with his principal clergy the Papal Court at Avignon. Robert ignored the summons and the Pope pronounced new excommunication against him, and against the Bishops of St. Andrews, Dunkeld, Aberdeen, and Moray. But the people of Scotland had grown tired of these vacant threats, this thunder without lightning, and a parliament sitting at Arbroath in April of that year addressed to the Pope a remonstrance notable for dignity beyond the common speech of parliaments, and for its heroic conception of the Christian promise to mankind.

After a preamble relating the oppressive acts of Edward I, it averred that ' at length it pleased God to restore us to liberty, from these innumerable calamities, by our most Serene Prince, King, and Lord, Robert, who for the delivering of his people and his own Rightful Inheritance from the Enemies' Hand, did like another Joshua or Maccabaeus, most cheerfully undergo all manner of toil, fatigue, hardship, and hazard. The Divine Providence, the right of succession by the Laws and Customs of the Kingdom (which we will defend till death) and the due and Lawful Consent and Assent of all the People made him our King and Prince. To him we are obliged and resolved to adhere in all things, both upon the account of his right and his own merit, as being the person who hath restored the people's safety, in defence of their liberties. But after all, if this Prince shall leave these principles he hath so nobly pursued, and consent that we or our Kingdom be subjected to the King or people of England, we will immediately endeavour to expel him, as our Enemy and as the subverter both of his own and our rights, and will make another king, who will defend our liberties. For so long as there shall but one hundred of us remain alive, we will never give consent to subject ourselves to the Dominion of the English. For it is not Glory, it is not Riches, neither is it Honour, but it is Liberty alone that we fight and contend for, which no Honest man will lose but with his life.'

' *Quia quamdiu centum vivi remanserint, nuncquam Anglorum dominio aliquatenus volumus subjugari,*' they wrote : ' *Non enim propter Gloriam, Devitias aut Honores pugnamus, sed propter Libertatem solum-*

modo, quam nemo bonus nisi simul cum vita amittit.'
The Latin is somewhat rugged and uncouth.
It has hardly the elegance of Cicero, the long
roll and suave rotundity of scholarship and
cultured senators : but in its rough honesty
there is the invincible spirit of a free people,
the stark determination with which Robert
had imbued his lieges and the land of Scotland.
Neither Pope nor temporal king had much
hope of prevailing against people who could
speak with such a tongue and breed such
thoughts.

XI

THE manifestation of this heroic spirit does not mean that Scotland had now become an embattled Utopia : parliament still had time and cause to pass Acts regulating such every-day matters as foreign trade and salmon-fishing, and in 1320 a conspiracy of some magnitude was discovered against King Robert, and a parliament at Scone, before which the conspirators were tried, became known, for the terror of its revelations and the severity of its sentences, as the Black Parliament. William de Soulis, a grandson of one of the Competitors, was the figure-head of the conspiracy—England was supposed to be in the background—and he and his coadjutor, the Countess of Strathearn, were punished with imprisonment for life, while their principal allies were condemned to the traitor's death by hanging and drawing and decapitation.

The Arbroath manifesto created a marked impression on the Papal Court, and the Pope now advised Edward to make a lasting peace with Scotland. But Edward preferred secret diplomacy—which was unsuccessful—and the Scots were endeavouring to conclude a private agreement with Edward's enemy, the Earl of Lancaster. This agreement was not ratified, and presently Lancaster was defeated, captured, and executed. Edward thereupon wrote to the Pope : ' Give yourself no further solicitude about a truce with the Scots ; the exigencies of my affairs inclined me formerly to listen to such proposals, but now I am resolved to establish peace by force of arms.'

The Scots anticipated this promised attack by raiding eighty miles into England ; Robert led one army, Douglas and Randolph the other ; they returned with some useful plunder, and prepared for the English invasion by making a desert of southern Scotland. Edward crossed the Border in August, 1322. So thoroughly had Robert cleared the country of crops, cattle, and goods, that an old bull, too lame to be driven off, was the only booty the English won. Famine impeded their advance, and dysentery reduced their strength. They lay three days in Edinburgh, and then withdrew. Douglas harried their retreat but could not prevent them from sacking the abbeys of Holyrood and Melrose and burning the monastery of Dryburgh.

Robert, having mobilised an army from the Highlands and Islands, retaliated by invading

England, and nearly succeeded in capturing Edward near Rievaulx Abbey in Yorkshire. The English were defeated there after a battle in which ' the Scots were so fierce and their chiefs so daring, and the English so badly cowed, that it was like a hare before greyhounds.' [1]

This new evidence of Edward's inability to defend his people persuaded Sir Andrew de Harcla, the heroic Governor and now the Earl of Carlisle and Warden of the Western March, to conclude a separate peace with King Robert, thinking ' that it would be better for the commonalty of both kingdoms that each king should possess his own without homage of any sort, than that such slaughter, conflagration, imprisonments, devastation, and depredation should go on every year. . . . The poor folk, middle class, and farmers in the northern parts were not a little delighted that the King of Scotland should freely possess his own kingdom on such terms that they themselves might live in peace.' [2] But Edward's view of the treaty was different from the farmers' view, and de Harcla was subsequently arrested and, with all possible degradation, executed for treason.

But Edward was again compelled to sue for peace, and on May 30, 1323, a truce of

[1] *Scalacronica.*   [2] Lanercost Chronicle.

154

thirteen years was proclaimed at York and ratified at Berwick. English intrigue at the Papal Court continued, however, but without much effect. Robert sent his own ambassador to Avignon — his nephew Randolph, Earl of Moray—and this daring and resolute soldier now showed a certain gift for diplomacy, and by tactful insistence on his own and King Robert's desire to fight for Christianity in the Holy Land, convinced the Pope that it would be desirable to recognise Robert as King of Scots. His Holiness, admitting the soldier's logic, consented to this courtesy and wrote at length to King Edward explaining his reasons for yielding : Edward replied with unconcealed displeasure. But negotiations proceeded for a permanent peace, and commercial relations between the two countries were slowly renewed.

In 1326 Randolph negotiated a defensive and offensive alliance with France : Randolph was rather out-generalled, however : it was agreed that either country should terminate any condition of peace with England in the event of the other being at war with England, and that the Scots should invade England whenever England should be at war with France. In the same year a parliament was convened at Cambuskenneth, in which for the first time representatives of the Scottish burghs sat with the barons and nobility : their principal duty was to vote a grant to the King of the tenth penny on all rents to compensate him for the depreciation of his revenue by prolonged expenditure on the war.

Edward II's unhappy reign was now drawing to a close. The baronial case against him was that he undertook ' nothing in the way of honour or prowess, but was only acting on the advice of Hugh le Despencer so as to become rich. . . . The commons of the time were wealthy and protected by strong laws, but the great men had ill will against him for his cruelty and the debauched life which he led.' [1] On the Feast of St. Hilary, in January, 1327, the Bishop of Hereford preached on the text from Ecclesiasticus, ' A foolish king shall ruin his people.' On the following day the Bishop of Winchester preached on a text from the story of Elisha and the Shunammite, ' My head, my head,' and explained with sorrow what a feeble head England had had for many years. On the third day, in the Great Hall at Westminster, the Archbishop of Canterbury took for his text, ' The voice of the people is the voice of God,' and announced that by unanimous consent of all the earls, barons, archbishops, bishops, clergy, and people of England, Edward was deposed from his

[1] *Scalacronica*.

pristine dignity, and that the prince Edward should succeed.

The succession of Edward III produced a new series of diplomatic interchanges, which succeeded only in irritating the Scots. The English offered to renew the truce which bore the authority of Edward II, and also proposed a treaty of more lasting peace. But as they still declined to acknowledge Robert's sovereignty their good faith was not unnaturally suspect. At the same time Henry de Percy was authorised to receive into the King of England's peace any Scots who desired that dubious benefit, and England was still intriguing against Scotland at the Papal Court. Edward Balliol, moreover, son of the puppet-king John Balliol, had three years before been brought back to England with great solemnity, and was living there in the state befitting an illustrious person. Robert would have required a very simple faith, a childish faith, to believe in the sincerity of England's peace offers : but he and his counsellors had long lost their innocence. On Edward III's coronation day the Scots made a hostile demonstration against Norham Castle, and plans were prepared once more to raid the northern parts of England unless peace were conceded on acceptable terms.

The new king and his advisers were given ample time to make ready a suitable reception for the invaders. A feudal levy was ordered, German mercenaries under John of Hainault were engaged, and a bright-hued flock of knights gathered from Flanders and Brabant, from Artois and even from Bohemia, to win renown in the first campaign of the boy-king whose ambition was to be the mirror of chivalry. This magnificent and motley army gathered at York, and tasted war without waiting for the Scots to come near them : for the English archers quarrelled with the foreigners, and such brawling started, and such ill-will grew between them, that for four weeks the knights of Hainault and Flanders and Bohemia could scarcely stir from their lodgings by day or doff their armour by night. But presently the English army, a great host, marched northwards out of York. Their progress was slow, and they came somewhat ponderously into Northumberland, ' a savage and a wild country full of deserts and mountains.' [1] At Newcastle lay another considerable force, and Carlisle was also heavily garrisoned. But neither the King nor his commander in Newcastle nor the Governor of Carlisle could get any information about the movements of the Scottish army, that, swiftly riding, came burning and

[1] Froissart.

spoiling and crossed the Tyne before news of them reached it. ' These Scottish men are right hardy,' says Froissart, ' for when they will enter into England, within a day and a night they will drive their whole host twenty-four miles, for they are all on horseback. They carry with them no carts, for the diversities of the mountains that they must pass through, in the country of Northumberland. They take with them no purveyance of bread nor wine, for their usage and soberness is such in time of war that they will pass in the journey a great long time with flesh half sodden, without bread, and drink of the river water without wine ; and they neither care for pots nor pans, for they seethe beasts in their own skins. They are ever sure to find plenty of beasts in the country that they will pass through. Therefore they carry with them none other purveyance, but on their horse : between the saddle and the pommel they truss a broad plate of metal, and behind the saddle they will have a little sack full of oatmeal, to the intent that when they have eaten of the sodden flesh that they lay this plate on the fire, and temper a little of the oatmeal : and when the plate is hot they cast of the thin paste thereon, and so make a little cake in manner of a cracknel or biscuit, and that they eat to comfort withal their stomachs. Wherefore it is no great marvel though they make greater journeys than other people do.'

The Scottish leaders were Randolph and Douglas : the King, though no longer in good health—he was suffering from a disease that has generally been described as leprosy—had with indefatigable spirit gone again into Ireland to examine the possibility of fomenting a new rebellion in Ulster [1] : but his hopes were defeated, and after some time he returned to Scotland, having accomplished nothing. Randolph and Douglas, however, were themselves masters of mobile warfare, and under their command the raiding army baffled and bewildered the portentous chivalry of England and Hainault. The smoke of burning houses would show where they were busy, but by the time the English had armed themselves, and paraded in their proper companies, and displayed their banners, the Scots were far away and new smoke told of fresh destruction. Once they left a rhyme stuck on a church-door to mock their slow-foot enemies :

> ' Longe beardes, hartelesse,
> Paynted hoodes, witlesse,
> Gaie cotes, gracelesse,
> Make Englande thriftlesse.'

It was decided that as the Scots would have to recross the Tyne to get home it would be

[1] Bain.

wise to wait for them by the ford they had already used, fourteen miles from Newcastle, and discarding the greater part of their baggage the English army hurriedly marched thither and lay there in great discomfort in bad weather by a flooded river. For a week they endured all manner of discomfort, for they had set out with no more food than each man could carry for himself, and when rations arrived from Newcastle, they were poor in quality, insufficient in quantity, and a penny loaf cost sixpence. Their harness rotted in the rain, their bivouacs of green branches made but a poor shelter, and all the wood was too wet to burn. And still they heard no word of the Scots, who were snugly encamped in Weardale.

The English decided to set out and look for them again, and a reward was offered of knighthood and lands worth £100 a year to any one who should bring news of the Scots' whereabouts. A dozen knights and squires set out in search of the enemy and their guerdon. For four days the English marched southwards, scarcely knowing why or whither, and then a squire called de Rokeby came in to say he had found the Scots, and indeed had been captured by them, but they, hearing of the reward he would win for finding them, and being, they said, also eager for battle, had released him and sent him back to his king. The English immediately followed de Rokeby and discovered the Scots in a strong position on high ground to the south of the River Wear. King Edward issued a formal challenge : let the Scots come down from their hill and fight fairly on level ground : the Scots, less chivalrous and having no more than a third of the English numbers, replied that they intended to stay where they were, and to stay as long as they pleased. At twilight they blew their trumpets as though ' all the devils of hell had been there,' [1] and they lay that night, still defiant, in the warmth of enormous camp-fires. For three days the armies faced each other across the river, and light skirmishing relieved the monotony of their watch. The Scots were short of rations, and starvation, it was hoped, might bring them to reason. But on the fourth morning they had vanished. In the darkness they had quietly withdrawn from their hill and found another position, two miles away, where woods and marshes protected them from attack. That night Douglas led two hundred horsemen on a sudden raid into the English camp, and nearly captured the King. Having roused the whole camp, he sounded the retreat and safely withdrew : Randolph asked how

[1] Froissart.

he had fared : ' Sir,' said Douglas, ' we have drawn blood.'

A day and a night of most discreet activity followed. The English were ill at ease and fearful of another raid when darkness fell. In the Scottish lines camp-fires burnt brightly, and behind the lines the Scottish army was silently going home by a wet road through the protecting marsh. In the morning the English again woke to find an empty camp before them : till mid-day they stood to arms, fearing a trick ; then they realised that the Scots had really gone, and their boy-king wept bitterly for his enemy's escape. It was no use to follow them. The campaign was over, and at York, on August 15, 1327, the magnificent army was ingloriously disbanded.

Froissart, describing the retreat of the English, says ' they were nigh so feeble that it should have been great pain for them to have gone any farther,' and though it is not quite clear whether he refers to the knights or merely to their horses, it is true that a weary inclination for rest, not merely from marching but from war, now became apparent in England. The Scots, however, showed no signs of fatigue. Robert had returned from Ireland, and brisk arrangements were made for a new campaign. Robert laid siege to Norham Castle ; Durham was raided ; Randolph and

Douglas, having invested Alnwick Castle, behaved with some levity and relieved the tedium of the siege with ' great jousts of war by formal agreement.' [1] Victory was assured, and they knew it, and now they could afford the time for a few tournaments.

The English parliament met at Lincoln. Depressed by the thought of having to pay their recent mercenaries from Hainault for services that had been signally unprofitable, and urged to pacific measures by Roger Mortimer, the Queen-mother's paramour, they agreed to offer Robert a marriage alliance between his son, the infant Prince David, and the Princess Joanna, King Edward's six-year-old sister. This proposal, signifying peace with honour, was delivered to King Robert under the walls of Norham Castle. The siege was abandoned, and negotiations began without more delay. This was victory indeed, for Joanna's dot was the recognition of Scotland's independence.

Edward summoned his parliament to York, and issued safe-conducts thither for Scottish commissioners and representatives. There, on March 1, 1328, a statement was published in which King Edward asserted that he did ' will and grant by these presents, for us, our heirs and successors whatsoever, with the common

[1] *Scalacronica.*

164

advice, assent, and consent of the prelates, princes, earls and barons, and the commons of our realm in our parliament, that the kingdom of Scotland within its own proper marches as they were held and maintained in the time of King Alexander of Scotland, last deceased, of good memory, shall be retained by our dearest ally and friend, the magnificent prince Lord Robert, by God's grace illustrious King of Scotland, and to his heirs and successors, separate in all things from the kingdom of England, whole, free, and undisturbed in perpetuity, without any kind of subjection, service, claim, or demand. And by these presents we renounce and demit to the King of Scotland, his heirs and successors, whatsoever right we or our predecessors have put forward in any way in byegone times to the aforesaid kingdom of Scotland.'

Subsequent to this proclamation a treaty was framed, concluded in Edinburgh on March 17, and ratified by the English parliament at Northampton on May 4. Provision was made for the royal alliance ; for the employment by England of her good offices on behalf of Scotland at the Papal Court ; for the adjustment of various disputes with regard to private property sequestrated during the war ; for the prohibition of Scottish intervention in Irish affairs ; for the payment by Scotland of an indemnity of 30,000 marks in respect of damage sustained by the northern counties of England ; for the restoration to Scotland of the Stone of Destiny ; for perpetual peace between the two kingdoms, subject to the eminently fair provision that if Scotland, according to the terms of its treaty with France, should find it necessary to make war in England, then England should be at liberty to make war in Scotland.

The marriage of Prince David and the Princess Joanna was celebrated at Berwick in July. Not all the clauses of the Treaty of Northampton were so scrupulously regarded, however, for the citizens of London refused to part with the Stone of Destiny, and the Scots do not appear to have paid the promised indemnity of 30,000 marks. But the infraction of peace treaties is not so rare a phenomenon as to deserve special comment. The treaty was, and remains, King Robert's patent of victory.

Eleven months later, by a bull dated at Avignon, June 13, 1329, Pope John XXII granted to Robert, the illustrious King of Scotland, and to his successors, the right to receive anointing and coronation. This right, conferring a sanctity that no civil ceremony or claim in primogeniture could bestow, had

never belonged to the Scottish kings since
Rome dispossessed the Church of St. Columba.
By it the Catholic Church acknowledged what
secular power had been forced to concede,
and the claims for which Robert had fought
so long received the sanction of the ultimate
power in Christendom.

But the promise of anointing oils came a
little too late : supreme unction had preceded them, for Robert had died six days
before the issue of the papal edict.

XII

A LITTLE evening of peace had preceded the King's death, and the record of his last days has room to tell of building a castle, and a house, and a ship to sail on the Clyde. He built his castle at Tarbet in Kintyre, where, two hundred and thirty years before, Magnus Barefoot's galley had been pulled across the heather to mark his dominion of Kintyre and the Isles : it was a strong castle but not luxurious, for in time of ceremony carpets of birch-boughs were laid. His house was at Cardross, near Dumbarton, where there was more comfort and some show of royal eccentricity : for as well as falcons he kept a lion in a cage, and planted a garden, and glass windows lit his painted rooms. A jester called Patrick was hired out of England, and the Constable's accounts show a generous expenditure on salmon and lampreys and wine. A good deal was spent on rigging the great ship he built, and at Tarbet he installed a goldsmith's atelier : in the red flush of the goldsmith's furnace, and in sunlight on the

Clyde, with the hills rising from the calm water, climbing and striding to the North—he had an autumn season to see them purple, one month of May to watch them grow green in peace—in those two lights, of craftsmanship and the inland sea, a last glimpse is caught of the great King.

He was in his fifty-fifth year when he died, and his Queen had predeceased him by a few months. A life of constant strain and much hardship had aged him prematurely. His body was embalmed and taken to Dunfermline, where it was buried. Two hundred and thirty years later the choir, transept, and monastery of Dunfermline were razed by the Reformers, and the place of his grave disappeared in the ruins. Prior to burial his heart had been taken from his body, embalmed, and closed in a silver casket. Two years after his death, Douglas, in obedience to his king's request, set out to carry it in war against the enemies of Christ and then to bury it by the Holy Sepulchre. He voyaged to Spain, where Alphonso of Castile was fighting against the Moors of Granada, and joined the Christian host. In a battle on the marches of Andalusia, thinking ' rather to be with the foremost than with the hindmost, he struck his horse with the spurs, and all his company also, and dashed into the battle of the king

of Granada, crying " Douglas, Douglas ! "
thinking the King of Spain and his host had
followed, but they did not ; wherefore he
was deceived, for the Spanish host stood still.
And so this gentle knight was enclosed, and
all his company, with the Saracens, whereas
he did marvels in arms, but finally he could
not endure, so that he and all his company
were slain. The which was great damage,
that the Spaniards would not rescue them.' [1]

Robert's heart was recovered and brought
home with Douglas's body. The one was laid
in Melrose Abbey, and the other in St. Bride's
Chapel of Douglas. The Good Sir James,
says Barbour, was not so handsome that we
need speak much of his beauty : his face was
somewhat gray, and he had black hair. He
had great bones, broad shoulders, and finely-
shaped limbs ; his body was well-made and
lean ; when he was blithe he was lovely, and
meek and sweet in company, but all-another
countenance he showed in battle. He spoke
with a slight lisp that suited him well, and
so deft was he in arms that after all his fighting
his face was unscarred. Of his loyalty, un-
failing courage, skill in war, and wisdom in
council, history tells in plain words, and the
magnanimity of his spirit has never been
questioned. Only great kings are served by

[1] Froissart.

such as Douglas : only the greatest would not find their glory dimmed by such a friend.

Of Sir James—lisping a little, dark-hued, lovely when blithe and terrible in battle—we can make something of a picture ; but Robert escapes us. Barbour says nothing of his appearance, and whether his features were as kingly as his life cannot be told. His physical strength was surely prodigious : only strong hands kept his head on his shoulders in the wilds of Galloway, and only a blacksmith's arm could have split de Bohun's helmet from the little height of a pony : but strength was allied to speed, for that swerve from de Bohun's path was quick as a matador's : ' In the art of fighting and in vigour of body, Robert had not his match in his time, in any land,' says Fordun.

He was greatly-thewed, then, and skilled in arms. He had the primal virtues. His countenance may or may not have been beautiful : it does not matter. He was a king, and his nature was the quintessence of kingliness. We have observed the devices, the seeming tergiversation of his early years : we have seen that they were kingly devices, that his tergiversation was like a hill road that turns and returns in slow certainty of reaching the summit. Had he died in the hills of Galloway, in his hide-and-seek days, there would have been room for debate upon the propriety of his shifting allegiance. But now there is none, for his achievement justifies all he did. From his youth he had believed in the justice of his claim to the throne ; perhaps he believed, from the beginning, that he and he alone was able to lead Scotland to the victory of independence ; great men see visions, and the greatest realise them. His strength of character was born in a narrow dynastic pride, but he grew great when his selfishness, by a kind of sublimation, turned to patriotism, and identifying Scotland's cause with his own he fought, planned, starved, and endured for Scotland. Making himself Scotland's king, he made Scotland a nation. It is hardly possible to separate the man from his country, for Scotland became his cause, and the whole land was filled with his spirit.

It is true that he made a mistake when he killed the Red Comyn : but how magnificently he atoned for it ! It is true that he behaved with wanton recklessness when he challenged de Bohun at Bannockburn : but with what perfection of soldierly talent he justified his self-confidence ! The hot temper, the gaiety-in-rashness, of his brother Edward, were clearly a family heritage : the blood of their hard-headed Norman sires had been well mixed with the blood of Celtic mothers ;

passion cohabited in their hearts with shrewd-
ness and determination ; the pride of one
race went hand-in-hand with the amiability
of the other ; self-advancement was drowned
in idealism : ' It is not Glory, it is not Riches,
neither is it Honour, but it is Liberty alone
that we fight and contend for ' :—the words
of the Arbroath parliament are the words of
King Robert's spirit. And his amiability—
the amiability of the Celt, that had ousted the
colder pride of the Norman—is often spoken
of, more often implied, and, indeed, clearly
proved by the history of his early struggles,
when he gathered a few friends and a few
hundred soldiers by the magnetism of his own
character : he was a genial man, a lovable
man, as well as a great man. No tyrant,
lonely and luckless as Robert often was, could
have saved his skin, much less have raised an
army among bold and broken men. He was a
good comrade before he became a good king,
and men loved him before they honoured him.

Of his statesmanship and his generalship
the story of his deeds has told enough. His
systematic reconquest of Scotland reveals a
master's strategy, and his domestic campaign
as well as his numerous adventures in the
north of England show absolute genius in their
conception of war in terms of rapid movement. The invention of the mobile schiltron

was his contribution to tactics, and Bannockburn proved his ability to use and control it.
His supreme gift for leadership is made apparent not only by the soldierly quality and
indefeasible spirit of his troops, but by the
ever-loyal co-operation of his lieutenants—men
of such singular force of character and out-
standing ability as Douglas, Randolph, and
Edward Bruce—and by the total absence of
jealousy and other dissension among them.
The essence of his statesmanship was a clear
conception of Scotland's right to independent
sovereignty, an unyielding determination to
achieve it, and his earnest desire for peace
as soon as the victory at Bannockburn had in
fact established such a sovereignty. The minor
attributes of a statesman, his social intelligence,
a gift of speech, a suavity of manner, may be
discovered in the story of his reception of the
papal messengers in 1317 [1] : he smiles upon
them, he is blandly non-compliant, he exposes
their want of logic, he is helpful with sug-
gestions that can be of no help whatever, and he
is most courteously intransigent. A diplomat,
one says, having read the story, and adds to
the picture of the hero-king the complication
of fine manners and a cultivated intelligence :
a pretty addition to his qualifications as a
guerilla chief.

[1] p. 144.

His gift for diplomacy, together with his royal generosity, is shown again in his dealings with the Earl of Ross and his nephew Randolph, both of whom he made his loyal friends after they had been his enemies, and whose friendship he magnificently rewarded. None of those who helped him had ever cause to complain of niggardly recognition of their services, for his bounty was profuse. To the Church, whose priests and bishops had always been his true friends and most daring allies, he showed a boundless liberality. The Scottish Church had helped him with heart and voice, in body and in spirit, and he rewarded it with open hands. He never forgot his friends, and often he forgave his enemies.

But it is hardly necessary to gloss the story and decorate the record of his deeds with comment and exclamation. Robert was of heroic stature, and a hero is best revealed in action : the simple tale of his achievements is enough. It is often difficult to see his features clearly—as of a giant striding through a forest—but the noise of his progress is loud and clear : and though sometimes when a little quietness falls—when he halts his army in dangerous country to save the life of a poor woman taken in childbirth ; or when the monks of Lanercost observe with surprise that his progress through Cumberland has been strangely merciful ; or when half his ragged army gather round him on Loch Lomondside to hear him tell stories of the Twelve Peers of France—though at such times it is pleasant to catch sight of his gentle aspect, the heroic vision is still the important one. He re-created a nation, he unified a people that has always shown a genius for disunion, he won for Scotland a few years of rarest triumph, and fighting one of the decisive battles of the world he achieved a victory whose name became his monument and the covenant of his people. That victory deserted them after his death is evidence of the unique quality of his leadership, and that they remained unconquered in spite of many defeats is proof of the indomitable spirit and stubborn pride he implanted in them.

BIBLIOGRAPHY

Bain. *Calendar of Documents.*
Barbour. *The Brus.*
Barron. *The Scottish War of Independence.*
Burton. *The History of Scotland.*
Cambridge Mediaeval History.
Fordun. *Chronica gentis Scotorum.*
Froissart. *Chronicles :* trans. Berners.
Gray of Heton. *Scalacronica :* trans. Maxwell.
Hailes. *Annals of Scotland.*
Lanercost Chronicle : trans. Maxwell.
Lang. *History of Scotland.*
Mackenzie. *The Battle of Bannockburn.*
Mackenzie. *The Bannockburn Myth.*
Maxwell. *Robert the Bruce.*
Morris. *Bannockburn.*
Rymer. *Foedera.*

INDEX

179

SHORT BIOGRAPHIES

5s. each

'Each separate volume is admirably produced, sensibly bound and illustrated, and available for the very moderate price of five shillings. As a publishing venture this series deserves unstinted praise. I urge all those who are as yet unacquainted with it to lose no time in repairing their omission. The Peter Davies series should become a popular habit.'

HAROLD NICOLSON in *The New Statesman and Nation.*

'Mr. Peter Davies has managed to do what no creator of a series of small biographies has succeeded in doing before— he has persuaded his authors to be authentic biographers without any nonsense. . . . In appearance and price these volumes are perfect.' HUGH WALPOLE.

'Apart from the matter of the volumes, which in every case is from an authoritative pen, this series is a thing of real beauty. The race of people cannot yet be quite extinct who love to handle and to look at books that are seemly, books which by their very outside appearance seem to pay respect at once to the business of a writer and to the business of a publisher.' *The British Weekly.*

JULIUS CAESAR By JOHN BUCHAN

'. . . nothing but praise is due to the candour, the sustained and balanced energy, and the dramatic skill of the book as a whole . . . it is hard to conceive a better presentation of a great historical subject within the limits of a short monograph.'
The Scotsman.

'Mr. Buchan tells his famous story tersely and well . . . he has given us, within a brief compass and in language which . . . is always vigorous and effective, an admirable bird's-eye view of a truly amazing career.'

E. E. KELLETT in *The Spectator*.

VOLTAIRE By ANDRÉ MAUROIS

'. . . light and well balanced, amusing and instructive.'
DESMOND MACCARTHY in *The Sunday Times*.

'A picture of Voltaire far more vivid than many a full-length biography.' *The Listener*.

MARLBOROUGH By The Hon. Sir JOHN FORTESCUE

'The narrative of the famous campaigns is such as one would expect from so accomplished a military historian. Clear and concise in style, and necessarily compressed in matter, it gives none the less a vivid picture.' *The Spectator*.

'Seldom have an author and a subject been better fitted to each other.' *The Glasgow Herald*.

MOZART By SACHEVERELL SITWELL

'Mr. Sitwell's book is admirable. No one has brought out more clearly the inner tragedy of Mozart's life.'

The Times.

'Mr. Sitwell's eager and breathless delight quickens our nerves like a glass of wine.'

CONSTANT LAMBERT in *The Referee*.

AKBAR By LAURENCE BINYON

'The insight of the poet and the knowledge of the Orientalist are most happily blended, and the reader will here find the most vivid portrait of the great Mogul Emperor that has yet been drawn in English.' *The Times Literary Supplement*.

'The result has been a really valuable contribution to Indian history . . . Mr. Binyon's charming style and his remarkable insight into the character of his hero.'

SIR DENISON ROSS in *The Observer*.

LENIN   By JAMES MAXTON

'Its merits are real and by no means only literary . . . there is something stimulating in the presentation.'

The Times Literary Supplement.

'It furnishes an admirable account of Lenin's life and of the development of his ideas. It does more than this . . . it supplies a very clear and intelligent outline of the history of the Russian revolution.'

MICHAEL FARBMAN in *The Week End Review*.

ST. PAUL   By WILFRED KNOX

'Has all that effect of a sensational revelation which always comes from treating a Biblical character like an ordinary historical personage.'

CLENNELL WILKINSON in *The London Mercury*.

'Mr. Knox treats his subject with admirable lucidity and breadth. . . . This is a memorable and fascinating volume.'

The Manchester Evening News.

LEONARDO DA VINCI   By CLIFFORD BAX

'Its mysterious and fascinating subject emerges as fascinating and almost as mysterious as before—which is quite as it should be.'   SYLVIA LYND in *Harper's Bazaar*.

'It is the merit of Mr. Clifford Bax's sketch that it attempts to reconstruct from the multitude of data a convincing figure of a great man.'   *The Observer*.

QUEEN ELIZABETH   By Mona Wilson

' Miss Wilson's purpose was not to re-write the history of the reign, but to recall the high purpose and vivid personality of the great Queen ; that she has done admirably.'

The Times Literary Supplement.

' This is, no doubt of it, a book that was wanted. It is brief and knowledgeable, and it allows contemporaries to speak for themselves.'

Helen Simpson in *The Review of Reviews.*

RUSKIN   By David Larg

' The most piquant biography of a great Victorian that has been published since Lytton Strachey first invented the genre. Not that justice could be done to Mr. Larg's art by describing him as an imitator of Strachey ; he is much more than that.'   *The Manchester Guardian.*

' How it all happened is told by Mr. Larg in a mosaic of intimations drawn with admirable cunning from the vast quarries of Ruskin's work . . . this admirable dramatisation and condensation, which leaves one eager to read more of what Mr. Larg can do.'   Rebecca West in *The Daily Telegraph.*

THE KING OF ROME   By R. McNair Wilson

' Mr. McNair Wilson's short but attractive study of the Napoleon who never reigned.'   *The Scotsman.*

' . . . a poignant picture of the ill-fated Napoleon's ill-fated son, a human story written with sympathy and under-standing.'   *The Manchester Evening News.*

WILLIAM OF ORANGE   By G. J. Renier

' Dr. Renier has written a brilliant but impartial sketch of a singular and arresting personality.'   *The Scotsman.*

' Dr. Renier's book should long remain the standard English life of William of Orange . . . it has struck a perfect balance between impressionism and compilation.'

The Birmingham Post.

PRINCE CHARLIE By COMPTON MACKENZIE

' A gem (that is, it has the beauty, the scale, and the inspiration of a fine intaglio).'

OSBERT BURDETT in *John o' London's Weekly.*

' It is, of course, beautifully written . . . Mr. Mackenzie has told it finely and in beautiful proportion.'

The Glasgow Evening News.

SOCRATES By Professor A. E. TAYLOR

' Professor Taylor tells that story . . . with the ability and knowledge which may be expected from so distinguished a philosopher and scholar.'

HAROLD DALE in *The Sunday Times.*

' Into less than 200 pages, a couple of hours' easy reading, Professor Taylor has compressed a masterpiece of portraiture and of philosophical exposition. No living English teacher of philosophy has a better command of words that convey his meaning.' *The Scotsman.*

MACAULAY By ARTHUR BRYANT

' This little biography is a skilful condensation of and selection from a great mass of material, and a just and lively presentation of the results of much study.'

ROSE MACAULAY in *The New Statesman and Nation.*

' Within its necessarily brief compass, Mr. Bryant has written an attractive, informed and sympathetic biography.'

The Week End Review.

MARK TWAIN By STEPHEN LEACOCK

'Mr. Leacock should convince his readers there is room for yet another book about the much be-written Mark Twain—at any rate with himself to write it.' *The Times.*

'It would be difficult to imagine a better equipped and more completely satisfying critic and biographer of Mark Twain than Stephen Leacock—the one man of this day worthy to wear Mark Twain's mantle.' *The Morning Post.*

GIBBON By G. M. YOUNG

'It is not only that the picture of the man at all stages of life is so vivid and amusing, but that it discloses such varied erudition, such balance of judgment, such penetration of thought.' J. C. SQUIRE in *The Daily Telegraph.*

'Mr. Young brought an already well-stored memory to his subject, as well as excellent judgment. His work is consequently of durable value.'

DESMOND MACCARTHY in *The Sunday Times.*

WESLEY By JAMES LAVER

'It is a serious and a sympathetic study of that burning life-long mission of the strenuous evangelist.'

J. C. SQUIRE in *The Daily Telegraph.*

'. . . an admirable study of the man ; it is sympathetic, intelligent, and so written that the reader with little knowledge of theological or ecclesiastical problems can understand Wesley's work.' RICHARD SUNNE in *Time and Tide.*

ST. AUGUSTINE By REBECCA WEST

'It is supremely invigorating to discover . . . a biography so bold, so pure, so richly garnished with observation and wise comment, as the life of St. Augustine by Rebecca West.'

LORNA REA in *The Daily Telegraph.*

'She has penetrated into the inner life of the great African Father with an insight as rare as it is accurate ; and for Augustine's background she has given a vivid picture of the Roman world.'

The Times Literary Supplement.

CECIL RHODES By WILLIAM PLOMER

'Mr. Plomer writes trenchantly as an intelligent man of to-day ; . . . We feel a mind working all the time.'

BONAMY DOBRÉE in *The New English Weekly.*

'It is terse, well-proportioned, and spirited.'

The Spectator.

CASANOVA By BONAMY DOBRÉE

'Mr. Dobrée . . . has done his work excellently, and in good prose.' J. C. SQUIRE in *The Sunday Times.*

'Casanova is at his best in Mr. Dobrée's pages : he lends him a glamour which it is not so easy to find in his auto-biography.' *The Saturday Review.*

OSCAR WILDE By G. J. RENIER

'I believe it to be the best volume yet in this excellent series. It is pre-eminently sane, just, and charitable. It is written by a man of good taste who is also a man of the world. The prose is simple and direct.'

COMPTON MACKENZIE in *The Daily Mail.*

'His account of Wilde's life and trial is admirable in its brevity, directness, and discretion.'

The New Statesman and Nation.

MARY QUEEN OF SCOTS By ERIC LINKLATER

'Mr. Linklater has cut straight to the heart of the problem ; he has also given us a new and reasonable interpretation of Mary's character ; and he has done all this in a hundred and fifty pages without sacrificing grace and wit of presentation.   It is an admirable feat.'

EDWIN MUIR in The Spectator.

' Mr. Linklater can make history live.   His style is so lively, his portraiture so vivid. . . .'

CAMPBELL DIXON in The Daily Telegraph.

RICHARD CŒUR DE LION
By CLENNELL WILKINSON

' He has succeeded in giving us an admirable, life-like portrait of a great man of action.'

R. STRACHEY in The New Statesman and Nation.

' Mr. Wilkinson has succeeded in giving us the soul of a man and the portrait of an epoch.'

SIR JOHN SQUIRE in The Sunday Times.

WILLIAM THE CONQUEROR
By HILAIRE BELLOC

' . . . brilliantly told, with that taut simplicity which is Mr. Belloc's narrative style at its best.'

JOHN BUCHAN in The Spectator.

' Mr. Belloc . . . was obviously the right man to add William the Conqueror to this series of short lives of great men.   The choice has certainly been justified.'

The Saturday Review.

HARUN AL RASHID   By H. ST. JOHN PHILBY

' . . . What Mr. Philby has set out to do he has done admirably.'   Sir E. DENISON ROSS in The Sunday Times.

' This compact volume is an ornament to a fine series, and well deserves its place on the shelf alongside Mr. Laurence Binyon's Akbar.'   A. T. WILSON in The Spectator.

QUEEN VICTORIA By Mona Wilson

' . . . an interpretation of Queen Victoria which is ingeniously shrewd and written with distinction.'
The Daily Telegraph.

' Miss Wilson's short biography is vivacious and satisfying, and gathers a momentum of conviction as it goes on.'
The Spectator.

SARAH BERNHARDT By Maurice Baring

' He does it so well that we almost seem to see and hear her still.' The Times Literary Supplement.

' Mr. Baring is carrying me off my feet. . . . But what a perfect piece of writing ! '
A. G. Macdonell in The Bystander.

HENRY VIII. By Helen Simpson

' Admirers of her work as a novelist will know that they can expect from Miss Simpson as a biographer fine qualities of style and attack.' Sunday Times.

' This is a good book, sane, scholarly and just ; a little masterpiece of compression and proportion.' Morning Post.

PETER DAVIES LIMITED
30 Henrietta Street, London, W.C. 2